DEATH COMES EASY

When Mitch Evans is ambushed, he manages to turn the tables on his attacker, wounding him and demanding an explanation. His would-be bushwhacker is merely a pawn — Latham Parry, foreman of the Bar JWM, is behind the murder attempt. For Mitch's brother Brad owns the Bar-B ranch, and Parry is ambitious: not only does he hope to seize the reins of the Bar JWM, but also aims to take over the Bar-B spread — by any means necessary . . .

WILL BLACK

DEATH COMES EASY

Complete and Unabridged

LINFORD
Leicester

First published in Great Britain in 2015 by
Robert Hale Limited
London

First Linford Edition
published 2017
by arrangement with
Robert Hale
an imprint of The Crowood Press
Wiltshire

A catalogue record for this book is available
from the British Library.

ISBN 978–1–4448–3196–2

Published by
F. A. Thorpe (Publishing)
Anstey, Leicestershire

Set by Words & Graphics Ltd.
Anstey, Leicestershire
Printed and bound in Great Britain by
T. J. International Ltd., Padstow, Cornwall

This book is printed on acid-free paper

To Ben and Cheryl and my brand new grandson, Reuben. With love.

1

The gunshot came out of the blue.

One minute the lone rider had been admiring the spring scenery in all its glory — cottonwoods in bud, yucca in bloom, ferrocactus with their red tops, looking as though they were on fire, and a wide variety of wild flowers.

In the distance the mountains of the Sierra Nevada rose majestically to embrace the brilliant blue of the cloudless sky.

The slug caught Mitch Evans in the left shoulder. It was a lucky shot, skimming off the bone before it could do any real damage.

Instinctively, Mitch threw himself to the right, grabbing his Winchester as he thudded to the ground. The jolt sent a spasm of sharp pain coursing through his body, but he ignored it.

He had to.

A second shot smashed into the ground beside him; he didn't flinch and didn't move a muscle. He knew his very survival lay in the next few minutes.

Whoever was shooting at him needed to be sure Mitch was dead, or at least, unconscious.

Straining his ears, he picked up the sound of pebbles falling down the bluff to his left and then the sound of boots crunching the soil as the bushwhacker made his way to his expected prize.

Mitch heard the lever action of a rifle loading another slug into the breech and he moved his right hand till he felt the butt of his Colt.

Easing back the hammer, he waited.

Sweat oozed from every pore in his body: some caused by the sun's heat, but most from the throbbing pain in his left shoulder.

Yet still he didn't move. He hadn't ridden all this way for it to end here.

He felt, rather than saw, a shadow move briefly across his eyes and knew his assailant was towering over him.

He knew for certain when he felt a boot nudge his body to see if he was conscious.

Then he made his move.

Faster than the eye could see, Mitch drew and fired. The slug caught his assailant in the kneecap, sending the man backwards — screaming.

Mitch managed to raise himself on one knee, his gun still trained on the figure writhing in agony and gripping his contorted leg above the knee, trying to stanch the blood.

Still on one knee, Mitch scanned the bluff before him, unsure if there was anyone else up there.

He saw no movement or telltale glint of sunlight reflecting off metal.

'So, you're alone, mister,' he gritted at the prostrate man.

The man didn't answer.

'You want the other knee shot off?' Mitch asked, cocking the Colt.

Sweat was pouring down the injured man's face and, from out of nowhere, flies began to land on the slowly spreading pool of blood beneath the man's leg.

He was panting heavily, his teeth gritted together as he fought to control the pain.

'Alone. I'm alone,' he managed to say.

Mitch stood up and scanned the territory, looking for his horse. He let out a piercing whistle and within minutes the sound of pounding hoofs could be heard as his mount returned.

Grabbing the reins, Mitch mounted up.

'You ain't leaving me here, are you?'

'You tell me what I need to know and we'll see,' Mitch said.

'What — what do you need to know?'

'Who you are. Why you tried to bushwhack me. And who sent you.'

The man didn't answer straight away. Beads of sweat from both the heat and the pain he was in ran down his face. The pool of blood surrounding his leg grew ever larger.

Mitch knew that unless he stanched the blood with a tourniquet soon, the man would simply bleed to death.

The man knew this as well.

'My name's Cal Morgan,' he eventually said.

'That's one question answered. Two to go,' Mitch stated.

'I work for the Bar JWM ranch.'

'Yeah, I know it, twenty miles from here,' Mitch said. 'So Josh Winters sent you?'

'No — not exactly.'

'Not exactly?'

'No.'

'You ain't got much time left, mister,' Mitch said.

'It was — it was Latham Parry.'

'An' who's he?' Mitch asked.

'He's Winters's foreman,' Morgan replied.

'Go on,' Mitch said flatly.

'Can we sort my leg out, mister? I'm losing a lot of blood here.'

Mitch considered the question for a few moments, deciding the man was desperate enough to keep telling the truth, so he dismounted.

He took off his bandanna and tied it tightly round the man's thigh.

'Best I can do,' Mitch said as he stood up. 'Now tell me the rest of the story.'

'That's all I know,' Morgan said, still through gritted teeth. 'I was given twenty dollars by Parry to shoot you. He gave no reason. And Parry is not the sort of man you refuse.'

'So you'd kill for twenty dollars?' Mitch couldn't hide his disgust.

'Mister, if I'd've refused Parry would have killed me for sure.'

'Ain't so sure I ain't gonna kill you,' Mitch replied.

The look on Morgan's face was one of resignation. 'I don't get to a doc soon, you won't have to,' he said through a wave of pain.

'Where's your horse?' Mitch asked.

'Behind the bluff.' Morgan pointed.

Without a word, Mitch mounted up and led his horse up the small slope, disappearing from view.

Morgan watched him leave, hoping it was to get his animal. At least mounted, if he could manage it, he'd have a chance to ride into town and get some doctoring.

Five minutes passed and Morgan was getting edgy. *Maybe the fella has ridden off,* he thought.

Sweat was pouring from him now, and the pain was almost unbearable. He was at the point of giving up all hope when Mitch returned, leading Morgan's horse.

After dismounting and ground hitching both animals Mitch removed his Stetson, wiped the sweatband and put it back on.

'I can't mount up on my own,' Morgan whined.

'I still want to know why you tried to bushwhack me,' Mitch said, resting his right hand on the butt of his pistol.

'I told you already.'

'You told me who sent you, but not why,' Mitch grated.

'I don't know why. I was just told to take you out.'

'That don't make no sense,' Mitch said. 'I've never been here before.'

Despite the pain, Cal asked: 'Where're you headed?'

'Got a telegram from my brother,

seems like he's got himself a whole mess o' trouble brewin' and needed some help.'

'Would that be Brad Evans?' Cal asked.

'You know him?'

'Sure; well, I know of him, he owns a spread just south of here, the Bar-B,' Cal replied.

'This got anything to do with your boss?'

'Honest, mister, I ain't sure. Ol' Josh is getting on in years, but a better boss you'd go a long way to find. It's Latham who's running the show, an' he ain't satisfied with just bein' a foreman, I can tell you that.'

'So it's land-grabbin', is it?' Mitch said almost to himself.

'Mister, I need to get to a doc, pronto.'

'OK. I'll help you mount up.' Mitch dismounted and stood behind the stricken man. 'When I lift you, stand on your good leg.'

'I won't be able to lift my right leg,' Cal said.

'Don't worry, I'll lift it for you.'

It took Mitch some effort to lift the

8

man aboard his pony. The wound in his shoulder hampered his movement, but eventually he got the man in his saddle.

'How far's the nearest town?' Mitch asked, mounting up himself.

'Calvary, it's about ten or twelve miles south-east of here.'

'OK. You lead the way, an' no funny stuff, you got that?'

'Mister, if'n I survive this, you won't see hair nor hide of me agen. I can't go back to the Bar JWM. Parry will kill me for sure.'

Doc Mayweather was a larger-than-life character. Large in every sense of the word. He stood six feet five inches in his stockinged feet and had a stomach you could fit a saddle on.

A large, purple-coloured nose was the main feature of his face, a testament to his love of whiskey. Deep-brown eyes, above which grew a forest of hairy eyebrows, which in turn led to a full head of dark-brown hair.

Deep-brown eyes stared over half-

9

spectacles at the two men who entered his surgery unannounced.

'He's got a leg shot,' Mitch said.

'He's hit in the shoulder,' Cal added.

'What in hell you boys been up to?' Mayweather bellowed, in a voice as big as his frame.

'Well, I shot his kneecap,' Mitch muttered.

'An' I nicked his shoulder,' Cal said, leaning heavily on Mitch.

'Playin' cowboys and Indians?' Mayweather laughed.

'I'm bleedin' to death here, Doc,' Cal said through clenched teeth.

'OK, OK. Let's get him on the table.' Mayweather grabbed Cal under the arm, and between them they laid Cal down.

Grabbing a large pair of scissors that looked more like shears, Mayweather began cutting Cal's denims straight up the middle.

'Dammit, Doc, them's the only pants I got!' Cal groaned.

'If'n I don't stop this bleedin' pretty damn quick you won't need two pants legs, mister.' Mayweather continued cutting.

Mitch sat in the corner of the surgery and rolled himself a cigarette. He was just about to strike a lucifer when Mayweather turned on him.

'You wanna kill yourself, go outside. I don't allow smoking in here.'

'Smoking's good for you, Doc, you know that,' Mitch countered.

'Tell that to your lungs, boy,' Mayweather replied. 'No smoking in here.'

Reluctantly, Mitch got to his feet and shuffled outside.

Although it was late in the day Mitch guessed it was around four in the afternoon: the sun still shone brightly in the west. There were no clouds, just a heat haze and the gold orb of the sun was impossible to look at unless you wanted to go blind.

Mitch lowered his gaze and looked about the small town. One street, and that was it. What breeze there was raised dust from the parched earth. Just another one-horse town. He guessed that

11

if it wasn't for the surrounding ranches Calvary wouldn't even exist.

There was a small saloon, a livery, a mercantile, which probably did the most business in town; a gun shop with a sign hanging off rope, swaying in the breeze: 'New and used and we repair 'em too'.

Apart from a small café the rest of the street was filled with wooden shacks, around ten or twelve, all exactly the same.

He saw no sign of a sheriff's office or jail. Must have no need, he thought.

Mitch finished his smoke and tossed the glowing butt into the street. Not a soul was visible and, if he didn't know better, he would have thought it was a ghost town.

The pain in his shoulder had subsided to a dull ache. It was stiff, but bearable. Turning, Mitch walked back into the doc's surgery.

'How's he doin', Doc?' Mitch asked.

'He'll live. I stopped the bleeding. He was lucky, the bullet missed the patella'— he saw the look on the two men's faces

12

— 'the kneecap, but sure made a mess of some ligaments. Can't repair them.'

'Will I be able to walk, Doc?' Cal asked.

'You'll be able to walk, but that leg ain't gonna bend no more. Be as stiff as a broom-pole.'

'Well, that's better than losing the leg,' Mitch piped up.

'You'll need to keep off that leg for at least a month. I'll lend you a crutch. Come back in a week and I'll change the dressings. That'll be twenty dollars,' Mayweather said. He turned and washed the blood off his hands.

'Heck, Doc, I ain't got no more'n ten dollars to my name,' Cal said, shamefaced.

'I'll take care of it,' Mitch said. 'Check my shoulder over, Doc, and I'll pay.'

'Mighty generous of you.' Cal looked relieved.

'Oh, you'll work for it. You got no place to go, so we'll head out to the Bar-B as soon as I'm fixed up,' Mitch said with a wry grin.

The wound in Mitch's left shoulder, although deep, was clean and the damage more painful than dangerous. The doc patched it up and put Mitch's arm in a sling.

'It'll be sore for a while and a tad stiff, but you should be OK within a couple of weeks. Try not to use the arm overly,' Mayweather said. 'That's twenty-five dollars all in, and I'll throw in a bottle of laudanum. Use it sparingly, OK?'

'Thanks, Doc,' both men said almost together.

'Could you give me a hand getting Cal into the saddle, Doc?'

'Sure thing.'

'There a hotel or boarding-house in town, Doc?' Mitch asked.

'Sure. Ellie-Rae sometimes lets a room out. It's over the café. She cooks a mighty fine steak pie, too. Tell her I sent you over.'

Once saddled, the two men bid the doc farewell and set off to the café.

'Fine pair we are,' Cal said, 'me with one leg and you with one arm.'

14

'Well at least we ain't dead,' Mitch replied.

'Yet,' Cal added.

2

Josh Winters was well aware he was losing control of both his foreman and his ranch.

Wheelchair-bound after a riding accident, he was totally reliant on his housekeeper, Maria Gonzalez, for his every need.

Latham Parry, the foreman, had collected a set of men more used to gunplay than herding cattle or busting broncos. He had big plans for the Bar JWM, and he was a ruthless killer and manipulator, who would let nothing get in his way.

His plan was simple and as old as the hills: get rid of the smaller ranches that surrounded the Bar JWM — by fair means or foul — and the word 'fair' was not in his vocabulary.

The Bar JWM extended across some 30,000 acres, situated between Lubbock to the north and Midland to the south, most of it prime grassland fed by the Colorado River.

Josh Winters had founded the ranch some thirty years ago, fighting off Indians and claim-jumpers, as well as the elements. Initially intending to breed and raise horses for the army as well as the surrounding towns, he soon saw the profit to be made from cattle.

Once established, with a small ranch house built, he sent for his childhood sweetheart, Anne-Marie, from Galveston on the banks of the Gulf of Mexico, to join him and become his wife.

But the stage she was on was raided by Indians between Houston and Waco. It was six months before Josh learned what had happened.

He never married, and had no heir to his ranch and vast fortune. Most of his original and faithful crew were either dead or in a worse state than he was. With his heart broken, he devoted all his energy into building up a herd. The ranch house was expanded and the herd grew. Soon his beef was in high demand and the regular drives to Abilene and Dallas earned him more money than he could ever spend.

Maria Gonzalez had crossed the Rio Grande at Del Rio when she was an eighteen-year-old, to escape both the poverty and the threat her parents had made that she would be sold and married to the highest bidder.

The journey was arduous as well as dangerous, but her desire to rule her own life and her strength of purpose saw her through. She slowly made her way to Odessa, getting any job she could to keep body and soul together. Eventually she reached Lubbock — and that was where Josh Winters found her.

Josh had driven his buckboard into Lubbock at around three in the afternoon. His plan was to pick up supplies, grab something to eat, and get back to the ranch before nightfall.

His supplies were ready and waiting for him, and the storekeeper and his lad helped him load the buckboard.

'Thanks, Jim,' Josh said to the store-keeper. He tossed a dollar to the lad who helped out after school.

'Gee, thanks mister,' the boy said, his eyes wide as he saw the gleaming coin in his hand.

'What's that new eatery like, Jim?' Josh asked.

'Mighty fine,' Jim replied. 'Best stew and dumplings I ever did eat, and the apple pie just melts in your mouth.'

'Sounds good to me,' Josh said. 'OK if I leave the buckboard here?'

'Sure,' Jim said. 'We'll keep an eye on it.'

'Thanks.'

Josh made his way down Main Street, slapping the trail dust off his clothes as he went.

It was then that he heard a muffled scream.

Josh stood stock still, trying to fathom where the sound had come from. He took his Stetson off and cocked his head to one side, trying to cut out the noises on the street.

The muffled scream came again, and Josh ducked down a side alley.

The shadows were deep and black but he could just make out the outlines of three figures, two men and a woman. Josh immediately drew his Colt.

'What in hell's goin' on here?' he shouted.

The struggling stopped briefly as a gruff and obviously drunk voice bellowed: 'Mind yer business, mister.'

'I'm making it my business,' Josh yelled. 'Let that woman go. *Now!*'

In the deep gloom of the alley Josh saw one man break free from the woman and, as his eyes had become used to the darkness, he saw him reach for his gun.

Josh didn't hesitate. He aimed low and hit the man in the leg before he could pull the trigger.

Immediately, the other man drew, but Josh held his fire as he still had hold of the woman and his pistol was pressed to her head.

'Don't do anything stupid, fella,' Josh cautioned. 'Take your pal and walk away.'

'Oh, I'm walking away all right, and this li'l filly is walking with me. You just go about your business, cowboy, an' no one will get hurt.'

'That ain't gonna happen, fella,' Josh said, his Colt held steady in his right hand.

'Jed,' the injured man croaked, 'let's just get out of here. I'm hurtin' real bad here.'

'Shut your mouth. I ain't backing down to no greenhorn.' As the man said this, his attention was momentarily taken away from Josh, and that was all Josh needed to make his play.

Maria seemed to sense that, one way or another, the situation was about to end. Instinctively, she stamped on her captor's foot as hard as she could. The man's gun arm dropped slightly and without a second's hesitation, Josh fired.

The .45 slug caught the man called Jed in the upper arm, shattering the humerus from the collarbone. The man screamed and stood in shock for a few seconds as he watched his right arm fall to the ground.

Maria slumped to the ground and, for an instant, Josh thought his shot had hit her.

Rushing to her side, he knelt and was relieved to see a small smile on her lips as her large brown eyes peered up at him.

'Thank you, *senõr*, you saved my life!'

That had been forty years ago and Maria had devoted her life to Josh Winters ever since.

Sitting in his wheelchair, Josh found himself dwelling more on the past than the present; the future didn't even enter his head.

Now that the trail drive had started, with 2,500 head of prime beefsteak on the hoof, the only hands left on the ranch were Parry's hand-picked men, or rather, men whom Clancy had selected for the next operation that Parry had in mind.

Latham Parry was outlining his plan for the raid on the Bar-B that night. 'Plan' was perhaps too grand a word for it.

Brad Evans was one of the many thorns Parry had in his side. The Bar-B was fine grazing land and Parry saw acquiring it as the first step to building his empire. Old man Winters was too old and too frail to stop him, and Parry knew his days were numbered. With no family to inherit the Bar JWM, Parry would simply take it over.

But Parry was not a patient man.

He'd already taken steps to ensure that Winters's time would be up soon.

Real soon.

3

Mitch reined in outside the café and tied his horse to the hitch rail.

'Hang on here, I'll go an' get us a room,' he said to Cal.

Cal nodded. Although the laudanum was beginning to work he was still in a lot of pain.

Mitch opened the door to the café and immediately the smell of food filled his nostrils. It was then that he realized he hadn't eaten for at least twelve hours: his belly was now reminding him of that fact.

The café was small: a quick glance and Mitch counted six tables, five of which were occupied. A red-headed woman approached him, wearing an apron. Her hair was piled high on her head and she looked him over with eyes as green as grass.

Hurriedly, Mitch took his Stetson off and held it in both hands in front of him.

24

'Only got pie and greens left, mister,' she said between ruby-red lips revealing teeth as white as snow.

Like a fool, Mitch stood there with his mouth open.

Ellie-Rae put her hands on her hips. 'You dumb, mister?'

'No. No I ain't. Sorry. I — well — I— pie and greens would be good. Great, I mean, yes. An' a room. Doc sent us over.'

'Us?' Ellie-Rae cocked an eyebrow, a faint trace of amusement on her face at Mitch's embarrassment.

'Sorry, ma'am, my, er, partner is outside. Got himself a bullet in the leg. I just wanted to make sure there was a room here for us before I help him down.'

'You say Doc Mayweather sent you over?' she asked.

'Yes, ma'am. He fixed up Cal's leg an' my shoulder.'

'How long you staying?'

'Just the one night, ma'am, if'n that's OK.' Mitch's stomach was still rumbling and he wasn't sure if it was all due to hunger, or being in the presence of a beautiful woman.

'Guess I can accommodate you, Mr ...?'

'Evans, ma'am. Mitch Evans.'

'You want feedin' too?'

'Oh, yes, ma'am. Ain't eaten in a while.'

'OK, get your partner, I'll rustle up some grub.'

'Thank you kindly, ma'am.'

'An' quit calling me 'ma'am'. Name's Ellie-Rae O'Hara.'

'Miss O'Hara,' Mitch said as he put his Stetson on the vacant table and went outside to get Cal.

Getting Cal off the horse was much easier than getting him on it. Using his crutch, Cal limped into the café and sat down heavily, his right leg stretched out rigid in front of him.

Ellie-Rae returned with two plates piled high with pie and greens, and a plate of fresh sourdough bread.

'Coffee'll be along in a minute,' she said. As she turned to go back into the kitchen she asked, 'So who shot you?'

26

Mitch jerked a thumb at Cal. 'He did.'

'And you?' Ellie-Rae asked Cal.

'He did.'

'That's just plain loco,' Ellie-Rae said, and vanished into the kitchen.

Cal Morgan's appearance in Calvary hadn't gone unnoticed. One of Parry's stooges, an old-timer called Will — no one knew his last name — watched as Cal and a stranger walked their horses to the doc's place.

Will spent most of his time swamping out the grandly named Palace Saloon: cleaning out the spittoons and collecting — and draining — glasses left unattended on the bartop or tables.

He also had the amazing knack of converting any nickels, dimes and the occasional dollar into rotgut.

He might be the town drunk and a laughing stock, but he was no fool. He recognized Cal straight away, and knew he was one of Parry's men. He could also see the blood on the man's leg.

Will licked his lips. Dollar signs flashed

into his eyes and he was consumed with a raging thirst.

Latham Parry might slip him a dollar or two for this information and already Will could see the bottle of rotgut and a shot glass in front of him.

Doc Mayweather was seated on his rocker drinking a glass of lemonade as Will ambled across the street in his direction.

'Evenin', Doc,' Will said affably. 'Been busy I see.'

'I got no chores for you, Will,' Doc said.

'I ain't after work, Doc. Jus' shootin' the breeze. What's ol' Cal bin up to?'

'Didn't know you knew him,' the doc said.

'Sure, sure I do. One o' Josh's men, ain't he? Don't know the other fella though. He new in these parts?'

'You seem mighty interested in them, Will. Now why would that be?'

'Aw, you know me, Doc, jus' makin' conversation, is all.'

'Well, to put you out of your misery the other fella is Brad Evans's brother,' the doc told him, and took a sip of lemonade.

28

'That so?' Will mused. 'That so. Well, Doc, better get back to my chores. The devil drives an' all that. Be seein' ya.'

Will ambled round to the rear of the saloon as fast as his bony old legs could carry him, to where the buckboard and pony were housed.

The saloon owner, Brett Larson, a not very successful ex-gambler, who had one lucky break when he won the Palace and then quit, had given Will carte blanche with the buckboard in lieu of payment as he used Will to make deliveries and collections of supplies.

Will hitched up the pony and headed out to the Bar JWM.

When Mitch and Cal had finished their meal and were relaxing with the last of the coffee, Ellie-Rae asked if they wanted anything else.

'Ma'am — sorry — Miss O'Hara, that sure was a mighty fine meal.' Mitch rubbed his now full stomach.

'Thank you. That'll be six dollars. Including the meal, bed and breakfast.'

'And worth every penny,' Cal added.

Mitch paid the bill and Ellie-Rae showed them to their room.

'Thank you, ma' — Miss O'Hara, a good night to you,' Mitch said, sounding far more formal than he intended.

The room was small but looked comfortable. Two single cots were on either side of a small table upon which stood an oil lamp. Against the opposite wall was a small dresser with a bowl and pitcher, and two towels, neatly folded, with a bar of soap on top.

Mitch unbuckled his gunbelt and hung it on the bedpost, placing his Stetson on top of that, then flopped down on to the bed.

Cal lowered himself down and sat on his bed, resting the crutch against the wall. He, too, unbuckled his gunbelt, then slowly lay back.

'Could you just lift my leg on to the bed, Mitch?'

'Sure thing,' Mitch replied.

Once he'd settled Cal, Mitch lay on his own bed and, without closing the drapes or lighting the oil lamp, both men fell into an untroubled sleep.

It would turn out to be the last one they had for a while.

It was close on midnight when Latham Parry got his small gang together. The men had coated their hands and faces with axle-grease and wore headbands with prominent feather-and-deerskin clothing. In the dark, they would easily be thought of as Indians.

To complete the ruse, each man had a quiver and a bow slung around his shoulders. There would, hopefully, be no gunplay tonight.

Silently, the seven horsemen, led by Parry, left the Bar JWM and headed for the Bar-B.

Such was the vastness of the country that it would take over an hour to reach their target, but they were in no hurry. There was very little light from the moon and that was ideal for their purpose.

The ride over the grasslands was easy;

all they had to do was follow the river and that would lead them straight to the Bar-B.

When they got to around 200 yards from the ranch house, Parry held up an arm. The men dismounted, spread out, and walked towards the silent and dark house.

Two of the men had oil-soaked cloth wrapped around their arrows. The plan was simple: burn Brad Evans and his family out.

Having loaded their bows, the two men sent their now flaming arrows towards the ranch house and watched the sparks fly as the arrows found their target.

Within minutes the dry wooden roof was ablaze, lighting up the dark sky with a flickering orange glow.

Their next target was the front door; two more blazing arrows thudded into the door and that, too, burst into flame.

Now there was no escape. Anyone in the house was doomed.

Maria Gonzalez was beside Josh Winters's

bed within seconds of hearing him coughing.

She'd heard the horsemen ride out and, peering through the drapes in her room, she saw what looked like a bunch of Indians.

Then the coughing had started.

Maria knew that Josh had very little time left, but the old man never complained and was always ready with a smile whenever she entered the room.

She poured him a glass of water and lifted his head as she put the glass to his lips.

The water soon soothed his throat and he smiled at Maria.

'I want you to know,' he said with a feeble, croaky voice, 'that I've left everything to you in my will. It's lodged with the lawyer, Amos Kline. He's a good man and an old friend. There's a copy of the will in my safe. You know the combination, so just let Amos know. He's in Lubbock; he'll help you with everything.'

He broke off with a coughing fit, then resumed:

'You must get rid of Parry and his cronies. I've given him too much leeway and I know he's up to no good. So look out for yourself.' He took her hand and gently squeezed it.

Maria, choking back tears she would never let him see, said nothing. There was nothing she could say to the old man she had loved for so long.

Josh closed his eyes and within seconds had fallen back to sleep.

Maria allowed a single tear to run down her face and silently left the room.

It took ten minutes for the ranch house roof to fall inwards. A giant ball of flame billowed into the night sky and wood sparks flew through the air, landing all around the destroyed house.

Soon, small flames sparked in the grassy areas and Latham Parry smiled.

As the roof caved in the door to the ranch house flew open. At first Parry thought the wind created by the collapsing roof had blown it open, but then he saw a sight he knew he'd never forget.

A figure stood in the doorway. It was completely engulfed in flames.

As Parry and his men looked on in horror, the figure began to walk towards them, the steps faltering until the ball of flame sank to its knees and eventually fell face down on the ground.

Parry was the first to recover.

'Guess we'll have no trouble from Evans now,' he said, with a smirk on his face. He took out a cigar, struck a lucifer and inhaled deeply.

4

Mitch woke up as the first rays of the sun broke over the eastern horizon. He couldn't remember the last time he'd slept in a bed, and boy, had he slept well!

He stood and stretched before peering through the drapes at the deserted street below.

He splashed water on his face, dried himself off and immediately put his gun-belt on.

Behind him, Cal woke up. He coughed a few times, then reached for his makings.

He pushed himself up on the bed and yawned as he rolled himself a cigarette. Lit it, inhaled, coughed once more, then said, ''Morning.'

''Mornin', sun's up,' Mitch said and opened the drapes.

A shaft of sunlight headed straight for Cal's face and he immediately raised a hand to shield his eyes.

'Goddamn! Ain't I in enough pain,' he bellowed, A cloud of smoke left his mouth as he spoke.

Mitch pulled one of the drapes across to cut the light out. He bent down, pulled out a piss-pot from beneath the bed and relieved himself.

'You need this?' he asked Cal.

'Well, if I didn't, I sure do now,' came the grumbled reply. Cal swung his good leg off the bed, then lifted the stiff one.

'Need a hand?' Mitch asked.

'I'd rather piss my pants!'

'Suit yourself. I'll check on breakfast,' Mitch said. He left the room, leaving Cal to his own devices.

Halfway down the stairs, the unmistakable smell of frying bacon alerted his taste buds.

''Morning, Miss O'Hara,' he said.

'Call me Ellie,' she said without turning round. 'Coffee's on the stove, help yourself. Bacon, eggs and home-made bread OK?'

'Couldn't want for more,' Mitch said as he poured a cup of coffee.

'Your partner awake?' Ellie asked.

'Yeah, he's, er, getting ready,' Mitch said.

'He'll need a hand,' she replied.

'No, he'll manage. We'll hear him hopping down soon.'

No sooner had Mitch spoken those words than they heard the thump, thump, thump of Cal coming down. Then a muffled curse as the kitchen door swung open.

'Ya might have helped me,' Cal grumbled.

'You said you'd rather —'

'I know what I said, but that was ...' Cal halted as he caught sight of Ellie-Rae. 'Sorry. 'Mornin', ma'am.'

'Sit yourself down, breakfast is ready,' she replied. 'I'll pour you a coffee.'

'Thank you kindly, ma'am,' Cal said. He plonked himself down at the table.

Mitch smiled to himself, noticing that she didn't ask Cal to call her Ellie.

Ellie placed two plates on the table. 'Help yourselves to coffee,' she said.

'Ain't you joinin' us, ma'am?' Cal asked.

'I got chores to do, mister. This place don't run itself.'

'We'll be outa your hair soon,' Mitch said.

'Where're you heading?' Ellie asked.

'Over to the Bar-B. My brother owns it,' Mitch replied.

'Brad Evans?' Ellie said.

'You know him?' Mitch sounded surprised.

'Sure, everyone knows Brad and his family. He stops by for coffee when he picks up his supplies,' Ellie said. 'Give him my best,' she added and left the kitchen.

The two men finished their breakfast, eating as if they hadn't eaten in days. Mitch stood and poured second cups of coffee for them both, then placed the pot back on the stove. He sat, brought out his makings and rolled a cigarette.

Inhaling deeply, he looked round the kitchen, noting how clean and tidy the place was. As he smoked his thoughts drifted to Ellie-Rae.

He wondered how she'd look with her long hair down instead of piled up in a bun. She sure was pretty. He'd never seen eyes as green as hers, and a figure as cute as … well, it sure was cute.

He pulled himself together, stubbed the cigarette out and stood up.

'I'll get the gear and horses together, it's time we headed out.'

Cal merely nodded; his leg was giving him some pain, so he took a swig of the laudanum.

'Don't take too much of that stuff,' Mitch advised.

'I ain't. Pain's a mite sore this morning is all,' Cal replied.

Fifteen minutes later Mitch returned. Ellie-Rae was washing dishes and Cal was where he had left him.

'We're ready to leave now, Ellie,' Mitch said, removing his Stetson. 'Thank you kindly for the room an' all.'

'You're welcome, Mitch,' she replied, turning to face him.

Mitch's heart raced as he stared into her eyes. Was there a spark there?

40

'Give my best to your brother,' she said.

'I will.'

'And call back any time you're passing.'

Mitch's face beamed as he replied, 'I sure will, I sure will.'

Fumbling, he helped Cal to his feet and led him outside to the waiting horses. It took a great deal of effort to get him mounted, but once he was in the saddle, Mitch wiped rhe sweat from his face and went back inside to get his hat.

Ellie-Rae was drying her hands as she looked up. Again. Mitch's heart beat faster and he knew his face was beginning to redden.

Say something, his brain told him, *anything!*

'Thank you again, Ellie. I might be back in a few days, if'n that's all right.'

'Sure. I'll be here.' She smiled at his embarrassment, noting his boyish charm. She looked deeply into his dark-brown eyes and Mitch thought his legs would give way.

'Safe journey, cowboy,' Ellie said.

Mitch put his Stetson on and smiled. He couldn't think of a damn thing to say.

He smiled, turned awkwardly, and went out to his horse as if in a dream.

Mitch mounted up and the two men rode off.

Unseen by them, Ellie stood in the doorway and watched them go.

Latham Parry and his men watched as the ranch house burned to the ground, leaving only the stone chimney stack standing, surrounded by blackened lumber.

Thick smoke bellowed skywards, blotting out the stars, and here and there flames licked hungrily at whatever would still burn.

Casually, Parry walked over to the charred body, which was still smouldering, and stared at the remains of Brad Evans.

Lifting a boot, he kicked the body over on to its back. A grinning, eyeless skull faced him, the mouth wide open in a silent scream.

Silently, Parry flicked his spent butt at the body and pushed his hat back on his head and an evil grin split his features.

Job done, he thought.

He turned and ambled back to his horse. Mounting up, he called out, 'OK, boys, let's hit the trail.'

He wheeled the nag's head round and set off back to the Bar JWM.

The men rode in silence; the full horror of what they had done was just beginning to sink in and they didn't share Parry's enthusiasm for such a foul deed.

They were gunnies, not bushwhackers.

The men had killed before, some many times, but always in a fair fight; man to man.

This was different. There was nothing fair about burning a man and his family to death, and it started to weigh heavily on their minds.

But, not that any of them would admit it, such was the power Parry had over them that they feared him. Each man knew that Parry would kill any or all of them at the drop of a hat just for the hell of it.

It was purely the money they were paid that kept them at the Bar JWM.

The eerie blue light of the moon gently gave way to a dull rosy red as the sun began to rise in the east and the men entered the Bar JWM compound.

Maria woke instantly at the sound of so many hoofs. She parted the drapes of her bedroom window and watched as six Indians dismounted.

Panic engulfed her briefly, until she recognized Parry. She watched them dismount, take off their headbands and feathers and then lead their mounts into the barn.

Parry stripped off his buckskins, revealing his usual garb: black shirt and pants.

Maria had a bad feeling about this.

But who to turn to?

5

Will Garrett, the town's seemingly compulsory drunk, spent the night in the buckboard.

Anxious as he was to get to the Bar JWM — he had visions of a handsome reward for his information — the lure of the bottle of rotgut whiskey was stronger.

He drank himself into oblivion. Even seated on the buckboard, he lost his balance, dropped the reins and fell to one side. He was out cold. Fortunately for him, the nag that was pulling the buckboard found a clump of grass and was content to stop and eat.

The early morning rays of the sun slapped into Will's face, jerking him awake. His head throbbed, his eyes were bleary and he wondered where the hell he was.

Time for a wake-up drink, he thought.

He opened the second of the two

bottles he had 'borrowed' from the saloon, and took a mouthful. The fiery liquid hit the back of his throat. He felt like he was swallowing a bucketful of coarse sand. It burned its way down to his empty stomach and Will shuddered as the effects hit his brain at the same moment.

Shaking his head and rubbing his eyes, Will looked around him for the first time and, slowly, remembered why he was here.

He had news for Latham Parry.

But what the hell was it?

He vaguely remembered brushing the boardwalk outside the saloon, the broom more of a crutch than anything else. Two men! He remembered two men.

Then it all came back to him. He grabbed the reins.

'Giddup,' he yelled, and, slowly, the buckboard inched forwards.

Mitch and Cal walked their horses along the trail that led to both the Bar-B and the Bar JWM before it split, the left trail leading to Mitch's brother's ranch.

The going was deliberately slow as Cal could only manage one foot in the stirrup, his other leg hung stiffly down the horse's side. It seemed every small jolt hit his bad knee against the hard leather of the Western saddle.

'I gotta hold up a while, Mitch,' Cal said. 'My leg sure is sore.'

'How long afore we reach the Bar-B?' Mitch asked.

'No more'n a couple of hours, I figure. Trail splits about two or three miles ahead.'

'OK, let's see what I can do about your leg,' Mitch said, and he dismounted.

'Keeps hitting the side of the saddle,' Cal explained.

Mitch thought for a while, then came up with a possible solution.

'Well, side-saddle is out of the question on a rigid saddle, so, although it might be a tad uncomfortable, let's try putting your bedroll under your leg, that'll clear it of the saddle.'

'Uncomfortable beats pain, I reckon,' Cal replied.

It took only a few minutes to secure the bedroll to Cal's leg, moving it free from the saddle.

'Hell, feels like I'm doin' the splits,' Cal moaned.

'Well, it won't bang against this hard leather, so stop your complaining. Let's ride!'

Maria was beside herself with worry.

She knew something bad had happened and there was no one she could tell. The only ranch hands nearby were Parry's men, the rest were out on the range preparing the herd for the drive.

Josh was in no condition to be told anything and, even if he wasn't so ill, Maria would not burden him with anything that might cause him further stress.

Neither could she ride into town and inform the sheriff: that would entail leaving Josh alone — and vulnerable. She wouldn't put anything past Latham Parry.

She would just have to bide her time and seize any opportunity to get help.

The buckboard carrying Will Garrett

pulled up outside the bunkhouse and Will fell rather than climbed down from the driver's seat. A plume of dust rose in the still air as Will slumped to the ground.

His senses were so numbed by the rotgut whiskey that he felt nothing. All he knew was that the fall had taken the wind out of him and he couldn't breathe properly for a few minutes.

Will did feel the boot that caught him on the thigh, though.

'What the hell you doin' here, ol' man?'

Will managed to get himself on his hands and knees, panting, trying to get his breath back.

'Got … a … message,' he managed to say.

'Spit it out, then,' the man said. 'Ain't got all day.'

'Ain't fer you,' Will spat. 'It's fer Mr Parry.'

'Spit it out, ol' man, 'less you don't want your kneecaps.'

'What the hell's this ruckus, Clancy?' Latham Parry shouted as he stormed out of the bunkhouse.

'Mr Parry —' Will began.

'What you want, Will?' Parry didn't like being woken up. 'It had better be important.'

'Sure makes a man thirsty gettin' out here,' Will said.

'You stink o' booze, old man. Get him some water, Clancy. A lot of water,' Parry said.

Clancy grinned as he got the inference. 'Sure thing, boss.'

Five minutes later Clancy returned with a bucket. 'Here ya go, ol' man, plenty here to drink.'

So saying he emptied the contents of the bucket over Will.

Will coughed and spluttered. 'Weren't no need fer that!'

'Say what you gotta say and git the hell out of here,' Parry said, standing menacingly over Will.

Scrambling to his feet, Will said, 'I figured you might be interested in what I see'd in town.'

'Old man, if'n you don't spit it out soon I'm gonna run out of patience.'

'Figured it must be worth the price of a bottle or two,' Will added.

Parry drew his Colt and cocked the hammer. 'I'll be the judge of that!'

Will hesitated for a mere second before saying: 'I saw Cal ride into town with a stranger, they was both wounded. I asked the doc who the stranger was.'

'And?' Parry said between gritted teeth.

'It was Brad Evans's brother.'

Almost imperceptibly, Parry's eyes narrowed and hardened, but Will saw his expression change and he smiled inwardly.

Wordlessly, Parry uncocked the Colt and reholstered it. He then reached into his vest pocket and withdrew two dollar coins, which he threw to the ground in front of Will.

'Now get your ass outa here,' Parry said and went back inside the bunkhouse. Clancy snorted and followed his boss.

Will grabbed the coins and clambered back on to the buckboard. All that was on his mind was the two bottles of rotgut the coins would buy.

Maria had watched the whole episode unfold and, although she couldn't hear what was being said, it was obvious from the outcome that the old man had passed on a message to Latham Parry that was of interest.

She quickly scribbled a note and rushed across the compound to catch Will before he left.

'Wait!' she called out, and Will reined in. 'Please give this note to Doctor Mayweather, it's urgent.'

Will put the note in his vest pocket. He didn't open it as he couldn't read. Maria smiled, and handed him a dollar coin.

Will's face broke into a wide grin. *Three* bottles, he thought as he tipped his hat and set off back to Calvary.

Latham Parry stood in the doorway of the bunkhouse, smoking, trying to calm his anger at what he thought of as a betrayal by Cal Morgan. Damn him to hell!

He inhaled deeply, then his attention was caught by the sight of Josh's housekeeper running across the courtyard. He watched as she slipped something into

Will's hand.

'Now what the hell?' Parry said out loud. 'Clancy, I got a job for you.'

Mitch and Cal were making steady progress along the trail. By now the sun was at its height and the heat was intense.

'Sure could do with a break,' Cal said. The effort of staying in the saddle was exhausting.

'OK. There's a clump of cottonwoods just off the trail, they'll give us some shade. I got bread an' beans and a whole bunch of coffee,' Mitch said. He pointed towards the trees, which were about a hundred yards off the trail.

'Sounds good to me,' Cal said; the relief in his voice was evident.

The two men walked their horses across the rough, knee-high grass and reined in under the cottonwoods.

A gentle breeze rustled the grassland and the shade afforded the men some relief. Mitch dismounted and helped Cal out of the saddle and up against one of the trees.

Cal sank gratefully to the ground and Mitch began gathering wood to build a fire. Within ten minutes he had the fire going and, with the coffee on to boil, they ate the beans cold, soaking them up with the bread. When they finished eating, Mitch poured the coffee and the two men rolled a quirly and relaxed.

Pretty soon, both men fell into a light slumber.

'You called me, boss?' Clancy said, pulling on his gunbelt.

'Yeah, that housekeeper woman just handed a note to ol'Will. I don't trust her none. Would be mighty handy to see what the note said.' Parry grinned. He didn't have to say more.

'On my way, boss.'

Clancy saddled up and rode out of the Bar JWM. Parry watched him leave with a grin on his face.

Maria watched him go, too, and a feeling of foreboding filled her.

Clancy was in no hurry. He wanted to catch up with Will on the open range, not on Bar JWM land, so for a while he set his horse to a walk. He even had time to roll a cigarette and enjoy the ride.

In the distance, Clancy could see the dust cloud sent up by the buckboard. In less than a mile Will would be off Bar JWM land. Clancy finished his cigarette, tossed it away and set his horse into a canter.

It didn't take long for Clancy to pull up alongside the buckboard.

Will had heard nothing of his approach: his mind was on rotgut, his eyes focused on the trail ahead. And his hearing wasn't what it used to be. So when Clancy showed up he nearly had palpitations.

'What the hell you sneakin' up on me for,' Will blustered. 'Damn near scart me half to death!'

'Hold your horses, old-timer. You got somethin' Mr Parry wants,' Clancy said, and Will noticed his right arm hanging down by his holster.

'Dang! He don't want his money back, do he?' Will was alarmed.

'You crazy galoot! You think I'd ride out

here for a lousy two dollars? The note. I want the note.'

'What note?' Will started to look worried.

Clancy drew his pistol and cocked the hammer. 'You want remindin'?'

'Oh, that note, it's just a message for Doc Mayweather, is all.' Will started to feel around with his right hand for the shotgun he kept by the seat. He felt the wooden stock and slid his hand up to the double hammers. Silently, he pulled one back and felt for the trigger guard.

Will might be treated as the town drunk and, sometimes, idiot, but he was no fool. He knew that whether he handed the note over or not, Clancy would kill him.

He wrapped his finger round the trigger and made his move.

Moving faster than anyone would have believed, Will brought up the shotgun and fired.

Clancy had been too complacent, treating the old man as if he was a fool, and was taken completely by surprise.

The speed at which the old man moved suddenly seemed to be in slow motion.

He was sure that, in that last final second of his life, as the shotgun blasted, he could see the 12-bore shot flying towards him. Clancy's last act was instinctive, pure reflex of a gunny.

In that last second of his life, he squeezed the trigger of the .45 as the shotgun pellets peppered his head and chest, the force at such close range knocking him backwards, head over heels, to land with a sickening crunch in the dirt.

Clancy's .45 slug caught old Will on the forehead, blowing the top of his skull clean off. The force of the slug sent him reeling into the back of the buckboard.

While Clancy's horse bolted, the old nag that pulled the buckboard merely stopped grazing and began to walk forwards.

He knew the way home.

6

Mitch was the first to wake up.

He pulled his Stetson off his eyes as he heard the creaking sound of wagon wheels and the jingling of harness.

Rubbing the sleep from his eyes, he began to focus a little.

Mitch sat bolt upright, gun already drawn as he looked at the empty buckboard slowly meandering down the trail towards Calvary.

Mitch stood, and aimed his gun at the buckboard. 'Cal, Cal, wake up and cover me.'

Cal woke with a start; so deep had he slept that for a moment he didn't even know where he was. His leg soon reminded him.

'What, what the —' he stuttered.

'Cover me, Cal. There's an empty wagon on the trail. I'm gonna check it out and I don't want any surprises.'

He handed Cal a Winchester. 'Ready?' he said.

'Ready,' Cal replied.

Coming more to his senses, Cal realized he recognized the buckboard and horse.

'Hold up, Mitch. That's the buckboard that belongs to the Palace Saloon! I'm sure of it. Ol' Will Garrett uses it for delivery and collection for his boss.'

'Well, it sure looks empty now,' Mitch said. 'Just cover me while I check it out, OK?'

'OK.'

Slowly, and keeping low, Mitch crept across the open land towards the trail. The nag pulling the buckboard seemed unconcerned as he made his way along the trail.

Reaching the back of the buckboard, gun raised, Mitch stood and peered into the rear of the wagon and damn near brought his beans and coffee up.

It took him a few minutes to regain his composure; he replaced his gun and ran to stop the horse, which seemed oblivious to everything except getting back to town.

Grabbing the reins, Mitch pulled the nag to one side of the trail and ground-hitched it; the animal seemed quite content to graze on the lusher grass.

'What is it, Mitch?' Cal called out as he saw the man lean on the side of the wagon, take his hat off and wipe his head with a bandanna.

'Dead man,' was all Mitch replied.

'Let me see,' Cal called out. 'Git me on my horse.'

Once astride his horse Cal rode to the wagon and peered inside.

'Geez! You coulda warned me!' Cal said as his horse skittered; the smell of blood filled its nostrils and the animal snorted.

'Steady boy,' Cal said and stroked the animal's neck.

'You recognize him? Or what's left of him?' Mitch asked.

Cal stared, as if transfixed, at the crumpled form of what used to be Will Garrett. With the top of his head missing and the wagon soaked in blood, it was still easy to tell who it was.

The bed of the wagon was a seething mass of flies and the stench of death overpowering.

'That's Will all right,' Cal said, covering his mouth and nose with his bandanna. 'Only two places he could have come from.'

Mitch gritted his teeth. 'Sure as eggs is eggs, it weren't from Brad's place.'

'We better get him buried afore buzzards start having a go,' Cal said. 'Poor critter didn't deserve this.'

'There's a spade attached to the side of the wagon. I'll start digging; ain't no way you can,' Mitch said and dismounted.

Maria knew, without a shadow of a doubt, that her note would never reach Doc Mayweather. What she feared was that her last hope of contacting anyone was sure to fail now, and she would be at the mercy of Latham Parry.

She was under siege, and she knew it. Her first priority was to protect Josh at

61

all costs — including with her own life.

First thing to do was make sure the ranch house was as impregnable as she could manage.

When Josh had designed and built the ranch house many years ago, no expense had been spared.

There was always a constant danger of Indian attacks in those days, and Josh ensured that his home would be as safe as he could make it.

Every window was barred, there was a front door and two rear doors, all equipped with double locks and sturdy wooden cross-bars. There was a large root cellar under the kitchen and a tunnel that ran for a hundred yards away from the house.

To this day, only he and Maria knew about the secret tunnel.

Even the roof was safe: wood was the conventional covering, but Josh had used imported slate tiles which were impervious to the flaming arrows of any Indian attack.

Maria locked and barred the front

door, then did the same with the two back doors. She then entered the study and opened the gun cabinet. She removed a Smith & Wesson handgun, two Winchesters, and boxes of ammunition, which she took through to the kitchen.

She loaded both rifles, then the sixgun, and arranged them on the kitchen table.

Her thoughts drifted to the many times she and Josh had sat at this table, talking and laughing and ...

She banished those thoughts and, taking the handgun with her, climbed the stairs to Josh's room.

Leaving the gun on a small table in the hall, she entered the darkened bedroom silently.

She was not sure if Josh was asleep or unconscious. His breathing was shallow and every time he breathed in there was a rattling sound. To Maria, it sounded like death was very near.

She leaned closer and kissed him gently on the cheek, then dipped the cloth into a bowl of iced water to mop his brow.

As Maria stared at his ashen face, a small smile seemed to escape his lips. Josh Winters breathed in, then out, in a slow laborious way. The man was fighting to stay alive.

In the sweltering heat, it took Mitch over an hour of hard digging before he had a hole deep enough to bury Will Garrett.

He hoped it was deep enough to prevent critters from digging him up.

Grabbing hold of Will's booted legs, he unceremoniously dragged him off the flatbed. There was no way he could lift him, his shoulder was still stiff and painful but more than that, the top half of Will's body was soaked in blood and being feasted on by flies.

'Sorry, old-timer,' Mitch said under his breath. 'But there ain't no way I can lift you.'

As the body hit the dirt, a scrap of paper fell from Will's vest pocket. Mitch lowered the dead man's legs and picked up the piece of paper.

'What ya got there?' Cal asked.

Mitch didn't reply straight away. He read the note.

'What is it, Mitch?' Cal asked again.

'Seems ol' Josh Winters is dying, an' this woman, er ...' He paused as he skimmed down the note to Maria's name. 'Maria thinks there's something bad going down.'

'If Winters is dyin', then Parry must be up to something,' Cal said.

'He reckon on takin' over the Bar JWM?' Mitch asked.

'I reckon he wants to take over the whole valley,' Cal said.

'Makes sense,' Mitch said. 'The telegram I got from my brother told me he had steers missing, coupla dozen at a time. Said he was having trouble with a neighbouring ranch, but didn't say who.'

'Only one it could be,' Cal said.

'I'll finish up here,' Mitch said, grabbing hold of Will's legs once more. 'Then we'll ride to the Bar-B.'

Mitch laid Will to rest as gently as he could in the grave and began covering him up.

There were no rocks to cover the grave, so Mitch tramped the bare earth down as much as he could and hoped Will would rest in peace.

He stood for a moment, his head bowed, leaning on the shovel, then, wiping his brow, he grabbed his Stetson and turned to Cal.

'You might find it easier to drive the wagon. At least you can stretch out your leg awhiles.'

'I'll try it,' Cal said, 'If'n you could give me a hand.'

'Sure thing,' Mitch said.

Mitch helped Cal out of the saddle and into the driver's seat of the buckboard.

'Hey,' Cal said, 'there's a shotgun here under the seat.' He lifted it up; the smell of cordite was strong. 'Been fired recently, too.'

Cal broke the stock and checked the empty cases. 'Both barrels, too.'

'Well, at least he put up a fight,' Mitch said.

Mitch's thoughts turned to his brother and his family. His chest tightened as imaginary scenarios raced through his brain.

Getting to the Bar-B became even more urgent.

The riderless horse cantered into the Bar JWM compound and walked straight to the trough. Drinking its fill, the horse calmly walked to the barn and the hay it knew was waiting there.

It was some thirty minutes later when a cowhand roughly shook Latham Parry awake in the bunkhouse.

'Boss, boss, wake up.'

Parry sat bolt upright, his Colt in his hand. 'What the hell —?' He blinked and his senses came alive.

'It's Clancy, boss,' the hand said.

Parry rubbed his face. 'What about him?'

'He ain't come back, boss.'

'You woke me up to tell me that?' Parry was almost incandescent.

'His horse is back, but he ain't on it,' the hand said in a shaky voice.

This woke Latham Parry up quicker

than a bucket of cold water. His mind was racing now. No way could that old drunk outgun Clancy, no way.

'Get some boys together, we're ridin' out!'

'Sure thing, boss.' The man hurried off, thankful for his life.

In less than ten minutes Latham Parry led four men out of the ranch and along the trail to Calvary. He knew they wouldn't need to ride that far.

Twenty minutes later, they found Clancy, or rather, what was left of him.

A dozen buzzards scattered as the riders approached. The sound of their flapping wings and raucous screeches filled the air as they rose skywards, angry at being disturbed.

Parry reined in and dismounted. He stood over the remains of Clancy.

Strong as his stomach was, Parry had to fight to keep the bile down. Clancy was almost unrecognizable facially. His eyes were gone, as was most of the soft flesh around them. Lips had disappeared, making him look like a grinning skull.

His shirt was ripped open and blood-soaked. Parry could see ribs showing where the buzzards had feasted, and flies began to swarm now the birds had disappeared.

The four hands sat silently atop their mounts until one asked, 'That Clancy, boss?'

Parry nodded. 'Can't tell from his face, but look at his boots.'

Clancy's predilection for hand-tooled boots was well known, especially the two-tone ones he wore now.

'Shall I go fetch a wagon, boss?' one of the men asked.

Parry nodded again. 'Yeah, we can't leave him here.'

The man wheeled his horse around and set off at a gallop back to the ranch, glad to get away.

Parry lit a cheroot and inhaled deeply. Right now he wished he had a bottle of whiskey.

He started to inspect the ground around the body. Most of it was chewed up by the fighting buzzards, but on the trail he saw the wheel-marks of a wagon.

And blood!

So, Parry thought, Clancy didn't go down without a fight!

There was a faint trail of blood leading away from the death scene.

Was Will dead or merely wounded?

One way or another, Parry knew he had to find out. If Will had made it to Calvary he knew his plans could be thwarted. It wouldn't take long for the law to become involved, and that would complicate matters considerably.

Parry looked at the three rannies, nervously sitting their mounts, and wondered which one he could trust the most. Clancy had been his right-hand man. Now he was gone.

Parry made up his mind.

Burt Haystack, although Parry was sure that wasn't his real name, stood around six feet eight inches. A giant of a man, pretty handy with a gun and deadly with his fists.

'Burt, a minute.'

Burt edged his horse over to Parry and dismounted. 'Boss?'

'I need a man I can trust. Can I trust you?' Parry asked.

'Do I get paid extra?' Burt said.

'As deputy foreman, yes.'

'Then you can trust me,' Burt said, and smiled, showing tobacco-stained teeth.

Parry looked up into the big man's eyes and, lowering his voice, told him about the note.

'I need you to ride into Calvary and keep your ears and eyes open. I have to know if Will made it there or not.'

'An' if he did?' Burt asked, knowing the answer.

'If he did, he's wounded an' there's only one doc in town. Chances are, Will would have passed the note to him. There ain't no law in Calvary, no telegraph office either and the nearest sheriff is a two-day ride away. Should be easy to make sure that note don't go no further.'

'I get the message,' Burt replied and, mounting up, said, 'I'll report back in a few hours, boss.'

Parry watched him go and thought, well, at least the man has savvy.

Latham Parry mounted up and ordered the remaining two rannies to wait for the buckboard and get Clancy back to the ranch. They'd bury him there.

Maria had busied herself in the house. There was never much housework needed, except for perpetual dusting, and she was able to keep her eye on the approach to the ranch.

She heated up a beef soup she'd made the day before and prepared to feed Josh. Or at least, try to.

She placed the bowl on a tray, climbed the stairs and entered the darkened bedroom.

Josh was still asleep, so she gently placed the tray on a small table and opened the thick drapes to let the sunlight in.

She watched as the buckboard came hurtling out of the barn. Immediately, she knew that something serious had happened.

She sighed, knowing that pretty soon all hell could break loose. She just wished she knew what!

She moved across the room to Josh's bed and began to mop his brow once more. His face was grey and he felt cold to the touch, but beads of sweat formed on his forehead. His breathing was much shallower than earlier, every breath an effort.

Josh's eyes flickered open. Maria saw they were a dull, almost lifeless grey. For a few seconds it seemed that Josh was confused, unsure of where he was. Then, slowly, that smile of his appeared on his face and, briefly, his eyes sparkled. Maria smiled back, hiding her fears and concern.

'I have some soup,' she said. 'If you can manage it.'

Josh shook his head. He reached for her hand and gripped it firmly. He gave her hand a gentle squeeze, as if saying goodbye.

Then he fell into a deep sleep.

Mitch and Cal reached the fork in the trail. Straight ahead lay the Bar JWM, the trail to the left led straight to the Bar-B.

'How far now, Cal?' Mitch asked.

'No more'n five miles,' he replied.

'Be good to get out of this heat,' Mitch said. 'A cool glass of lemonade wouldn't go amiss either.'

'I could do with a beer,' Cal grinned.

The land either side of the trail was lush grassland for as far as the eye could see. Here and there small clumps of cotton-woods added to the beauty of the land. A clear blue sky was a perfect backdrop. The whole scene almost took Mitch's breath away. He rolled a cigarette as he walked his horse and felt at peace with the world.

Pretty soon they reached an ornately carved wooden arch bearing the name of the ranch, and at almost the same time Mitch caught the smell of smoke. At first he assumed the stove had been lit. Then, in the distance, he saw a thin spiral of white smoke hanging lazily in the air.

Mitch suddenly lost interest in his cigarette and flicked it away.

'Follow on, Cal, I'm gonna check that smoke out,' he said, concern evident in his voice.

Without waiting for a reply, Mitch spurred his horse into a gallop. As he neared the still smouldering building, he reined in and, with a sense of foreboding, walked the horse forward slowly.

The house had burned to the ground; the only part of it still standing was the stone chimney stack.

'Jesus!' Mitch muttered under his breath as he walked towards the ruin.

Then he stopped in his tracks.

Lying on the ground at his feet was the charred remains of what used to be a human being.

It was lying face down, arms outstretched. The hands were mere stumps with fingers burned off.

Mitch was violently sick. The sight and the smell of burnt flesh lingered in the air and it was more than he could take.

He fell to his knees. He was sure the body that lay before him was that of his brother.

Taking a deep breath, he filled his lungs with air in an effort not to be sick again. He needed to turn the body over to confirm his suspicions. He rose to his feet, reached inside his saddle-bags and brought out a pair of gloves.

Kneeling once more, he grabbed hold of an arm and pulled. To his disgust, the arm came away from the body and for a second or two, Mitch could neither move nor let go of the arm.

Then he flung it from him, as if it was still on fire.

At that moment Cal arrived. Shock was written all over his face as he saw the arm fly through the air.

'What the hell? Is that —?' He stopped, knowing the answer to his own question.

'I need to make sure,' Mitch said, his voice quivering.

Placing one hand under the chest and the other by the hips, he turned the body over as gently as he could.

The front of the body wasn't as badly burned as the back, Mitch guessed the ground had stopped most of the burning.

He saw the watch chain straight away and, pulling, he revealed a Hunter pocket watch — the one their father had given Brad.

Mitch stood, head bowed as he stared at the watch in the palm of his hand.

Cal got himself down off the buckboard and grabbed the crutch Doc Mayweather had given him.

He stood beside Mitch, unsure of what to say, so he said nothing.

Suddenly, Mitch started towards the smoking embers of the house, screaming.

'Julia, Julia!'

As fast as he could, Cal limped back to the wagon and grabbed the shovel. He couldn't think of anything else to do.

Mitch stood and stared at the remains of the small ranch house, fighting back tears.

'Maybe his wife —' Cal began.

'She's either dead, or the Indians took her,' Mitch said, finding it hard to control the tremor in his voice.

'Indians? There ain't been Indians round here for months,' Cal said.

Mitch pointed. 'There's arrows in the dirt, the ones that missed the house.'

Cal walked towards the nearest arrow and pulled it out of the ground. He studied it for a few moments, then said, 'This ain't no Indian arrow. I seen these before.'

'What?'

'Parry figured we were wasting too many slugs shooting at cans and such, so we set up a target and shot arrows. These arrows, I recognize the feathers.'

Anger began to well up in Mitch as this information sank in. He grabbed the shovel and stomped into the smouldering embers. He had to find out if Julia and baby Jon were in there someplace.

'I'll check the outbuildings,' Cal said. He didn't want to be around if Brad's wife and child were found burned to death.

Burt Haystack cantered down the trail. Sign was easy to follow, the wagon wheels had left deep ruts in the sand.

It was as he reached the fork that he reined in and scratched his head.

What the hell? he thought.

The sign he was following continued on towards Calvary, but there were fresher tracks coming back this way and taking the trail to the Bar-B.

Had the old man changed his mind? Burt was with Parry when they torched the ranch house, so if the old man had gone there, there would be no help for his wound — if indeed he was wounded.

Haystack was a slow thinker. Should he ride back to the Bar JWM and report to Parry? Or ride down towards the Bar-B?

He dismounted and checked the sign more thoroughly. This time, he could tell there were three horses: the nag that pulled the buckboard, easy to spot because one of its hoofs had recently lost a shoe, and two others; judging by the depth of the hoofmarks one was mounted, the other not.

Haystack's brain was turning over laboriously as he tried to decide what to do.

If he went back empty-handed and with no idea whether the old man was alive or dead, Parry would go mad.

Haystack wasn't exactly afraid of Parry;

in a straight fight Haystack had no match in the art of fisticuffs. But he knew Parry was not a fair man, and he'd seen him use those twin Colts he always wore, so it would never be a fair fight, man to man.

On the other hand, if he rode the trail to the Bar-B he might find out what was going on, or be shot dead for trying.

He was stuck between a rock and a hard place.

But maybe, he thought, there was a third option?

A slow thinker he might be, but Haystack was no fool. He decided to follow the wagon's tracks towards Calvary. That way, he reasoned, he could find out where, and maybe why, the buckboard had done a U-turn.

With his mind eventually made up, Haystack mounted up and set off down the trail.

7

Latham Parry was becoming more and more agitated as the time ticked past slowly.

The more agitated he became, the more his anger built up. He paced back and forth inside the bunkhouse, and the men not out on the prairie gave him a wide berth. Each man knew that Parry could vent his anger on any one of them for any or no reason at all.

He lit yet another cigarette and then poured coffee into his tin mug, but spat it out. The brew had stewed and the bitter taste only added to his anger. He grabbed hold of the coffee pot and flung it across the room, where it crashed into the wall, splattering coffee everywhere.

He stormed outside and bellowed, 'Beefsteak, git in here and sort this mess out!'

Beefsteak, who doubled as camp cook

and odd-job man, left the corral fence he was mending and made his way to the bunkhouse. He avoided looking directly at Parry for fear of making the man even more annoyed than he already was.

'And git some fresh coffee on, that stuff ain't fit for a coyote to drink.'

'Yes, sir, right away, boss,' Beefsteak mumbled, and entered the bunkhouse.

He retrieved the coffee pot, but couldn't find the lid. He eased his old bones down on to the floor, then, getting on all fours, he crawled around, peering under the bunks until he found the lid.

Parry was still outside and every man jack in and around the corral and barn area made themselves scarce.

'There ain't no sign of any —' Cal stopped, he didn't want to say 'bodies'.

'I'll check the barn,' Mitch said and ran across the small compound. More in hope than certainty he entered, but he already knew they wouldn't be there.

Slowly, he made his way back to the

burned-out ranch house and stood beside Cal.

'Mitch, no one could have survived this fire.' Cal placed a hand on Mitch's shoulder.

'So where are the remains?' Mitch said. 'There must be something.'

Mitch started to walk through the ash, kicking it up as he went, searching for any trace of his sister-in-law and nephew.

Suddenly, Mitch disappeared. This was missed by Cal, who was scanning the skyline. When he turned back, there was no Mitch visible.

'Mitch? Mitch? Where are you?' Cal called out.

There was no reply.

Burt Haystack had set his mount into a trot, following the wheel tracks towards Calvary, then he reined in. He'd reached the point of the trail where the buckboard had stopped and the two unknown riders had met it.

Burt dismounted and studied the ground. Dried red and black stains were visible on the soft sand, and to his left he saw where something bloody had been dragged through it. Drawing his gun, he followed the path.

The path stopped abruptly at a rectangle of freshly dug soil.

Studying the surrounding area, Burt saw that, to one side of the grave, where soil had been piled prior to filling in the hole, there were two sets of boot prints — and something else.

Small round circles that were deeper than the boot prints.

Burt's slow-moving brain began to work out the sequence of events, and he breathed a sigh of relief. He had something definite to tell Parry.

He grabbed his canteen and took a few swigs. It wasn't exactly filled with water. Contrary to ranch rules, his canteen only contained whiskey. Without it, Haystack couldn't function. He replaced the stopper on his canteen, hung it on the cantle and mounted up.

Spurring his horse, he set off back to the Bar JWM.

Summoning up all his energy, a sense of panic and foreboding filling him, Cal too stepped into the charred remains of the ranch house.

'Mitch?' he called out again, but there was still no reply.

Then he saw it.

A gaping black hole in the centre of the rubble. He looked down, but it was pitch black; puffs of smoke rose lazily into the air.

'Mitch, goddammit! You hear me?'

There was a low groan and Cal thought he saw movement.

'Mitch, you OK?'

A stunned Mitch sat up and rubbed the back of his head. It took him a few minutes to orientate himself. He shook his head and said, 'Yeah, I'm OK.'

Relief flooded through Cal's body. 'I'll get a rope, soon have you outa there,' Cal said.

Mitch struck a match.

It was then that he saw them.

Huddled in a corner, the baby still

clasped in her arms, sat Julia, her eyes closed. She looked serene, almost as if she was taking a short sleep, but Mitch knew she was dead. As was baby Jon.

A thousand thoughts rushed through Mitch's brain as he stared in horror. Brad must have sent them down here, to keep them safe, but he hadn't figured on the smoke!

The match burned down and Mitch felt the pain as it burned his fingers. He struck another and crawled across the floor of the root cellar. He had to make sure. Just in case.

His shoulder was throbbing again, Mitch thought he must have landed on it in his fall. He felt a warm sensation on his arm and knew the wound had opened up.

Ignoring the pain, he reached Julia's side, blew the match out and struck another. Placing his fingers on her neck, he felt for a pulse.

His head sank on to his chest and an involuntary sob escaped his mouth as he felt nothing. Just cool skin on a slender neck.

He was too late.

He was too late to help his brother, too late to help his wife and child.

Anger surged through his body, directed initially at Cal. If he hadn't delayed him, Mitch knew he could have helped Brad. Then at the unknown Latham Parry who, he knew instinctively, was behind this.

'I got a rope, Mitch,' Cal called down.

'Forget it,' Mitch said, through gritted teeth, trying to get his voice even. 'There's a ladder down here.'

'Are they ... are they down there?' Cal asked tentatively.

'Yeah. Yeah, they're down here.'

'Are they —?'

'Stop asking dumb questions. They're both dead, OK?' Mitch's anger was too strong to contain.

Cal took a step back from the cellar door and drew his breath in sharply. He knew he was partly responsible for what had happened, if only he ... Mitch's head appeared from the root cellar, but Cal couldn't look him in the eye.

'I'm sorry, Mitch. This is all my fault,' Cal managed to say.

Mitch didn't reply straight away. He climbed out of the hole, brushed himself down and was at a loss as what to do.

He looked at Cal. The man was genuinely upset and, for all his anger, Mitch couldn't really blame him.

'I wouldn't blame you for killin' me right now,' Cal said.

'I ain't gonna kill ya,' Mitch said and walked over to his mount. He grabbed his canteen, took mighty gulps, then poured the remaining water over his head.

'We need to get them on to the wagon and into town,' Mitch said, more to himself than Cal. 'There's some horse blankets in the barn.'

'I'll get 'em,' Cal said, glad to be doing something.

Mitch lit a cigarette and inhaled deeply, noticing how much his hand shook as he brought the cigarette to his lips.

It took five minutes for Cal to return, carrying the blankets.

'I'll bring them up,' was all Mitch said

and he climbed down the ladder. 'Spread the blanket out on the open ground,' he ordered.

Cal did as he was told. Within a few moments Mitch had prised the baby from his mother's arms and carried him up the ladder.

'Here, take baby Jon. Gently!'

Cal took the small bundle; a tear coursed down his cheek as he laid the baby on the blanket and covered up the little body.

Julia took a mite longer. In the cool root cellar, rigor mortis had set in, so Mitch had to carry her cradled in his arms which made it difficult to climb the ladder.

'Can you reach down, Cal?' Mitch called out.

'Sure.' Cal dropped his crutch, knelt on his good knee and placed his hands under Julia's arms. As he took her weight from Mitch momentarily, Mitch was able to push her up and clear of the root cellar.

He took her body from Cal and laid her down on a blanket. He took one last look, then covered her up and lifted her on to the buckboard. Cal brought the baby over and together they laid him by his mother.

Neither man was looking forward to their next task.

Brad.

Both men walked over to the remains of Brad Evans and stared once more in horror at the blackened frame.

Mitch laid the blanket next to the body, then walked over to where he had tossed the arm, picked it up and placed it beside the blanket.

'I reckon we try and roll him on to the blanket,' Mitch said. 'I ain't sure he'd stay in one piece if we try and lift him. You hold his legs and I'll take the head and torso,' Mitch added.

'OK? On the count of three: one, two, three!'

Together, both men rolled the body on to the blanket without losing any more limbs. Mitch placed the arm beside his brother and quickly covered him up.

Again, Mitch took the head and torso

and Cal the legs and they gently lifted the body from the ground. It was surprisingly light.

With all three bodies now on the buckboard, Cal retrieved his crutch and scrambled on to the driver's seat.

'Let's move,' Mitch said.

He'd deal with Latham Parry when his family had been laid to rest in Calvary.

Burt Haystack was feeling pretty pleased with himself as he set his horse into a gentle trot.

So pleased was he that he reached behind him and grabbed the canteen from the cantle. Another little nip would do no harm; besides, he deserved it.

He set the horse to a walk, pulled the stopper out with his teeth and raised the canteen to his lips. He felt the liquid slide down his throat and hit his stomach with a slight burning sensation. It wasn't the best quality whiskey, but it wasn't the cheap stuff either.

The feeling was good and, despite the heat of the late afternoon, he began to feel the warm glow creep through his body.

Without warning the horse suddenly stumbled, its front left hoof sank into a small hole on the trail, and it lurched to one side. Haystack was caught unprepared, only loosely holding the reins with one hand and the canteen pressed to his lips; he tumbled forward and somersaulted over the animal's neck, landing heavily on the ground.

With the wind knocked out of him, Haystack stayed where he was, fighting to get his breath back. He still held the canteen and hadn't spilled a drop.

Gradually, his breathing became easier and he sat up. His first thought was to put the stopper back on the canteen, but first he took another slug. Then he looked at his horse, hoping it hadn't broken a leg.

The animal stood quite calmly beside the trail, grazing and seemingly unhurt.

As he hauled himself to his feet, Haystack staggered and lurched, only just managing to regain his balance.

He'd drunk more than he intended,

but it felt good and he grinned stupidly to himself.

'Ol' Parry won't like that. No siree! Won't like that one bit,' he said out loud, and staggered sideways.

He giggled again as he reached for the reins.

Big as he was, Haystack had his Achilles heel.

It was contained in his canteen.

After three unsuccessful attempts at getting his right foot into the stirrup, he succeeded at the fourth and hefted his huge bulk into the saddle.

Swaying slightly, he spurred the animal on.

Having fed and watered the horses, Mitch and Cal set off for Calvary. The late afternoon sun still beat down, and the heat from the ground rose in gentle spirals, mirages danced before their eyes as they headed for the fork in the trail.

They reached the fork without incident, Mitch keeping an eye on their gruesome cargo, his thoughts whirling as he thought of his dead brother and family.

It was Cal who noticed the fresh tracks. One horse, which was carrying a heavy load judging by the depth of the hoofprints.

'Mitch,' Cal called out. 'Seems there's been a lone horseman down here recently.'

Mitch was brought back to reality: 'Huh?'

'Look yonder,' Cal said.

Mitch saw the tracks, but dismissed them as he saw in the distance a dust cloud, and it was coming their way.

'Seems there's someone coming this way,' Mitch said, pointing.

Cal reined in and peered ahead, but the figure was too distant to make out who it might be.

'Sure as eggs is eggs it's a Bar JWM rider,' Cal said. He picked up the Winchester and cocked it. He placed it across his lap — in readiness.

Mitch reached into his saddle-bag and brought out an old army telescope.

Through it he could make out the features of the rider.

'Sure is a big fella,' he said, and handed the 'scope to Cal.

Cal grunted. 'Damn!' he said.

'Recognize him?' Mitch asked.

'Yeah. It's Burt Haystack, one of Parry's henchmen.'

'He's on a recce, sure enough,' Mitch said as he took the 'scope back. 'Parry must want this note real bad.'

'Whatever he's planning started with your brother and his family,' Cal said. 'He must be getting ready to take over the Bar JWM, an' if ol' man Winters is on his last legs, Parry won't want any outsiders interfering.'

Mitch put the spyglass to his eye once more and peered at the oncoming rider.

'He's taken out his rifle,' Mitch said. 'Get down behind the footboard, Cal.'

A shot rang out; fortunately for the two men Haystack was as good with a rifle as he was with a Colt. His aim was so wide Mitch didn't even hear the bullet.

Mitch jumped to the ground as Cal

took hold of his Winchester and they both returned fire.

Haystack dismounted as quickly as his huge frame would allow and landed heavily in the hard-packed sand of the trail.

Lying flat on his stomach, Haystack sighted down the barrel of his rifle and started shooting again, his aim no better than it was before.

The distance between him and the buckboard was no more than a hundred yards, well within range of the Winchester, but Haystack could not get a shot anywhere near: overshooting, undershooting and sending wild wide shots.

'Hold fire, Cal,' Mitch shouted. 'He couldn't hit the side of a barn from ten paces.'

'We can't stay here for ever,' Cal said.

'Cover me, Cal. I'm gonna make my way over yonder.' He pointed to his right. 'We might catch him in crossfire.'

'OK. But keep low; he's a lousy shot but he might get a lucky one in,' Cal said.

'Lucky? Sure wouldn't be lucky for

me,' Mitch said and started towards the tall grassland to the right of the trail.

Once off the trail Mitch was completely hidden by the grass. The only thing Cal could see was the grass moving as Mitch made his way.

He began firing at Haystack again, keeping the man low on the ground. There was no return fire. Even Haystack realized he had no chance of hitting anyone.

Using the covering fire, Mitch made a wide arc through the grass until he felt he was somewhere to the right of Haystack; then, stooping, he raised his head high enough to get a clear view.

His guess had been a good one. He was no more than fifteen feet away. He ducked down. Now he had his bearings.

Cal had lost sight of Mitch, but he made sporadic shots to keep Haystack busy.

Mitch decided to talk first, and shoot only if necessary.

'Throw down your weapons, Haystack, and stand up real slow with your hands in the air where I can see them.'

Silence.

'One last chance, Haystack,' Mitch yelled.

Then Mitch heard the distinctive sound of a rifle being cocked, ready to shoot.

'Give it up, man. I've no wish to kill you, but I will if you try anything.' Mitch waited.

He didn't have to wait long.

A slug hissed past his left ear and Mitch dived to the ground.

He chambered his Winchester and waited for Cal to provide covering fire. When he did, Mitch jumped up and loosed off two quick shots.

After the second, he heard a deep grunt.

Mitch cocked the rifle for a third time but held his fire.

The eerie silence was only broken by the warm breeze rustling the tall grass.

'You see anything, Cal?' Mitch called out.

'Nope, he ain't moving,' Cal responded.

Mitch tentatively got to his haunches,

rifle ready, then raised his head above the grass. He could see Haystack clearly — and the blood.

Mitch stood and walked the short distance to the giant man's body, his rifle hanging loosely by his side.

Blood was oozing from the right side of Haystack's stomach. There were two wounds, and Mitch knew both his shots had found their target.

Flies were already starting to buzz around the pool of dark blood and Mitch used his Stetson to swat them.

Then he heard a groan. The man was still alive — barely — but alive.

Mitch waved to Cal, beckoning him to bring the buckboard down.

Within minutes Cal drew up in a cloud of choking dust.

'Goddammit, Cal!' Mitch said, coughing and pulling up his bandanna over his nose.

Cal ignored the remark and both men waited for the dust to settle.

'He ain't dead yet,' Mitch said.

Cal clambered off the wagon and stood

beside the body of Burt Haystack. 'Hell,' he said. 'What're we gonna do?'

'Beats me,' Mitch said. 'I ain't no doc and there's no way we can load him on the wagon.'

'We'll have to leave him here,' Cal said. 'We ain't got no choice.'

'We can't do that,' Mitch said.

'What d'you suggest, then? It'd take four or five men to lift that hulk off the ground. I got one good leg an' you got one arm.'

Without replying, Mitch walked over to Haystack's mount and gave it a mighty whack on the rump. The startled animal, who had been content to munch on the grass and was grateful not to have its giant master on its back, set off in a frenzied gallop.

'What the hell?' Cal started.

'If his mount gets back to the Bar JWM riderless, they'll send a hunting party out to investigate,' Mitch said. 'That way, I figure we can leave him here.'

'Let's git outa here,' Cal said. He mounted the buckboard. Mitch could see he was moving a lot easier now and he too mounted up.

'Let's go,' Mitch said. They set off for Calvary in silence.

Latham Parry had his trusty band of men in the bunkhouse. He was getting impatient, waiting for Burt Haystack to return. He had to know what was going on and what was in that note.

His first thoughts were to rush the ranch house and force Maria to tell him, but he knew she'd die before she betrayed the old man. No, he'd have to wait.

But he wouldn't wait long.

8

Maria was beside herself with worry. Josh Winters was more unconscious than asleep and she needed the doctor out here as soon as possible.

The ranch house was practically impregnable — Josh had seen to that in the early days; the only way anyone could get in was with an axe through one of the walls, and it seemed unlikely that anyone would try that.

There was a plentiful supply of food in the root cellar beneath the kitchen, and salt beef in abundance. The kitchen had its own water pump so, if a siege situation developed, she knew she could hold out until help came.

She also knew that Josh couldn't.

Maria gently lifted the old man's head and plumped up the pillows before lowering him. As she bathed his forehead with cold water Maria's attention was caught by noises out in the courtyard.

She moved to the window, pulled one of the drapes slightly apart and peered out through the barred window.

It was late afternoon and the shadows were lengthening; thin fingers of black seemed to be devouring the land near the western horizon.

In the courtyard, she could see six or seven men clustered round a horse. She had no idea to whom the horse belonged, but there seemed to be a lot of animated conversation going on — most of it coming from the ranch foreman, Latham Parry.

The ranch house was at least 200 yards from the barn. At that distance it was impossible to hear what was being said but, whatever it was, it wasn't good news.

Parry was all but stamping his feet like a spoilt child and the ranch hands were visibly drawing back from him.

It seemed as though Parry was barking out orders as, suddenly, six men ran towards the barn. Five minutes later they thundered out and hit the trail to town.

Parry slapped his thigh with his

crumpled derby and led the horse into the stables.

Maria quietly closed the drapes and wondered what on earth was going on. She was certain it had something to do with Will Garrett and the note she thought she had surreptitiously passed to him. If Parry got that note ...

Maria silently slipped out of Josh's bedroom and made her way down to the study. There, she sorted through her keys and found the one she was looking for.

She unlocked the gun cabinet and stood back.

There were four of the latest Winchester rifles and a Sharps, all fixed upright side by side. On one shelf was a selection of handguns, mostly Colts, and below that, another shelf stacked with boxes of ammunition.

At the base of the cabinet was a drawer with two heavy brass handles. Maria slid the drawer open and removed an ornately hand-tooled holster.

She removed it and smiled at the memories it brought back, as the smell of leather filled her nostrils.

Josh had bought it for her and insisted she learn to use both a handgun and a rifle. With the gunbelt he'd also purchased a pearl-handled Colt and silver-plated Winchester, both .45 calibre.

It had not taken Josh long to discover that she was a natural. Not a fast draw, but extremely accurate: she could out-shoot him with her eyes shut.

The gunbelt had been made especially for her slim waist and she slipped it on, then loaded her Colt and holstered it. She hadn't worn the gun rig for a good few years and she was aware of the weight on her hips.

She then took hold of the silver-plated Winchester and loaded that, too. She took out four boxes of ammunition, containing in all 200 bullets; she thought this a bit excessive, but better safe than sorry, and she carried them through to the kitchen.

She poured herself a coffee, sat at the kitchen table and waited.

Mitch and Cal could see the lights of Calvary in the distance. Early evening dusk was beginning to fall, but Cal knew they'd reach town before it got dark.

Mitch had been silent since the incident with Haystack, his thoughts now on his brother, sister-in-law and his nephew. He was also pondering the note he had in his vest pocket.

He had no proof, except Cal's confession and the arrow, that Latham Parry was behind this, but his gut reaction told him the man was evil and needed to be stopped.

The question was, how?

There was no law in Calvary, the nearest peace officer was over a hundred miles to the east, and the chances of a US marshal passing through town seemed pretty remote.

So deep was he in thought that he failed to hear the thunder of hoofs approaching rapidly from the rear.

But he heard the gunshot.

The slug thudded into the back of the buckboard.

'Shee-it!' Cal yelled. 'I guess they found Haystack!'

'Looks that way,' Mitch said, pulling out his rifle and jumping to the ground.

'We can't outrun 'em, Cal. Keep low and commence to shootin'.'

So saying, the two men set off a volley of shots. In the distance they could see two riders, who immediately reined in, sending up a cloud of dust that obscured the view from all four men.

Then, silence.

'You see 'em, Cal?' Mitch called out.

'Too much dust, wait till it settles,' Cal replied.

Two more shots rang out, too close for comfort.

Mitch saw the flashes as the rifles were fired. 'They've split up, Cal,' he called. 'You take the one on the left, I'll take the right.'

'OK,' Cal said and concentrated his vision to the left of the trail. The grassland here was much shorter, so cover was harder to find.

Another shot rang out and Mitch

aimed at the gun flash. Immediately, he heard a deep groan. Whoever was out there had been hit, that was for sure. Mitch began to belly-crawl to the left of the trail to see if he could do the same with the second bushwhacker.

Cal was firing blindly: the light was fading as the sun sank ever deeper. A red glow, bloodlike, bathed the scene as Mitch sighted down the rifle's barrel, looking for any sign of movement.

His patience was rewarded.

Slightly to his left he saw the gun flash, Cal saw it as well and both men fired almost simultaneously.

The two men waited.

There was no return fire.

'Cover me, Cal,' Mitch almost whispered. He got to his knees and peered ahead. He could see no movement, but he did see a dull red glow as the dying rays of the sun reflected off something metallic.

Mitch crawled forwards until he could see the owner of the rifle. The man didn't move. Mitch waited a few moments then, keeping low, he walked towards the body.

The man lying on the ground didn't move a muscle, Mitch could see blood on the man's shoulder and was about to lower his rifle when the man made his move.

Bringing up the Winchester with one hand, the man prepared to fire. But he was too slow; Mitch triggered off a single shot. It took the top of the man's head off. Blood gushed like a fountain for a minute or two and the body slumped back flat to the ground.

Cal had dropped to the ground and hobbled over to Mitch. 'You OK?' he asked.

'Yeah, almost had me fooled there, playing possum. Let's check the other guy.' Mitch, followed by Cal, walked towards the other body.

'Goddamn!' Mitch exclaimed. 'He's gone!'

Jed Jones, the second rider, had had his skull creased by Mitch's Winchester;

another half-inch to the left and his brains would have been spattered over the prairie.

He lay unconscious for a few minutes. He came to with the sound of gunfire filling his ears.

In the murky half-light he looked across to where his partner should be, but all he saw was a man walking, crouched low, with a rifle in his hands. Jed knew there was nothing he could do as two quick shots were fired.

The man with the rifle was standing upright now and Jed knew his partner was dead. If he didn't move soon, he'd be next.

His cow pony was less than ten feet away, munching on the rich grass; it took more than a few gunshots to rattle the old mare.

Jed gave a low whistle. The horse's ears pricked up as he lifted his head and looked in Jed's direction.

'Come here, you mangy ol' cur,' Jed whispered.

The horse ambled over as if it had all

the time in the world. Jed checked the two men on the other side of the trail, but they were preoccupied. His partner was obviously dead or badly wounded; either way there was nothing Jed could do.

Jed grabbed the reins and, as quietly as he could, walked the animal as far away as it took for him to feel safe enough to mount up.

With the light failing quickly now, it was becoming increasingly difficult to see the two men, but he sure as hell recognized one of them: Cal Morgan!

Jed swung into the saddle; his head was spinning and his vision was slightly blurred as he dug his heels into the horse's flanks. The soft sand and grass muffled the sound of its hoofs. He knew that the boss would want to know what had gone on.

Latham Parry could no longer control his anger. The news that Jed had brought back was worse than he had feared.

So, the man he'd sent to kill Brad Evans's brother was now fighting on the brother's side! Damn the man. Damn him to hell!

Seething, Parry told his men to saddle up.

'What about Haystack? We never made it to Calvary to get the doc,' Jed said. Immediately he regretted opening his mouth.

'The hell with Haystack, he can take care of himself. We gotta stop that wagon reaching town.' Parry stormed off to the barn to get his horse.

'I ain't too happy with this,' Jed said. 'Burning down the Evans place was bad enough; hell knows what he's up to next.'

'We're in too deep now,' one of the men said.

'Yeah, an' you know the boss will never let you ride outa here alive,' added another.

'We best saddle up, I guess,' Jed said, reluctantly.

'Better get Chow to patch your head up first. He's over at the cookhouse.'

'OK. Wait up for me,' Jed said and dragged himself off to the cookhouse.

Maria stood in the front parlour watching the scene in the courtyard. Again, she couldn't hear what was being said, but it was obvious by Latham Parry's antics that whatever he had planned had failed again. Maybe Will Garret had made it to Calvary after all!

Her hope was renewed.

'We best get moving,' Cal said. 'If'n he gets back to the Bar JWM, Parry is bound to send out his gang; there's more men than we can handle alone.'

'Guess you're right,' Mitch replied. 'Let's go.'

They set off at a faster pace, the distant lights becoming brighter and brighter as they neared and the evening drew on.

After only thirty minutes, they entered town. As usual, it was quiet. Cal pulled the wagon to a halt outside Doc Mayweather's house and wearily dismounted.

Mitch was already knocking on the doc's front door.

The door creaked open and a surprised Mayweather eyed his visitors.

'Didn't expect to see you boys back so soon,' he said. 'Come in, come in.'

Mitch stood his ground. 'Are there enough men in town you trust?' Mitch asked.

'Trust? Well, sure, but why?'

'I got four bodies in the wagon, Doc. My brother and his wife and child, and an old-timer name of Garrett.'

'My God! What on earth —'

'There ain't time to explain it all, Doc. We need to get these bodies somewhere decent and gather some men together, men who can use a gun.'

'I've a stretcher in the surgery, I'll get it now,' the doc said. He disappeared inside.

Mitch had no wish to reveal the bodies of his family so, keeping them covered, he and the doc carried them inside one by one. Will Garrett being the last, the only one not covered up.

When they'd finished that gruesome task, the doc said: 'Now give me some idea of what's going on.'

114

Mitch relayed his story, keeping it as short as possible, then fished in his vest pocket and handed the doc the note they'd found on Will Garrett's body.

> Doctor Mayweather. Mr Josh is dying before my eyes. I beg you to come to the Bar JWM as soon as possible.
> I fear there is something evil going on outside. I have secured the ranch house against any intrusion. Whatever is going on, Latham Parry is behind it.
> Maria.

Mitch showed Mayweather the arrow he had found at the Bar-B.

'Cal said this is an arrow that the hands use for target practice, to save on bullets.'

'I've heard that, too,' the doc agreed. 'Right, get that wagon off the street an' I'll go see our town mayor. We'll organize ourselves.'

'You have a mayor?' Cal's surprise was evident in his voice.

'We got a town council, too,' the doc replied. He turned to leave, but Mitch grabbed his arm.

'I fear Parry and his boys might well be heading to town as we speak. We were attacked twice on the way here and Parry is bound to want to know what that note said.'

'Then I shall hurry,' the doc replied, alarm clear in his voice.

'I'll take the wagon to the saloon barn,' Cal said, 'and feed this mangy critter.'

'No,' Mitch almost shouted. 'Take the horse, but leave the wagon. We might need a barricade.'

'Good thinking,' Cal said, and began to unhitch the horse.

Latham Parry was a man possessed. He'd been patiently planning his takeover of the Bar JWM and surrounding areas for nearly three years and he wasn't about to let a low-life ranny and saddlebum stop him.

It had taken him ten years to track down his brother, Larry. What he found was a shell of man, more dead than alive, living in a disused line shack in the middle of nowhere.

His brother's only contact with the outside world was a trapper who called in periodically with vittles and moonshine.

His mind had gone. It took three weeks for Latham to find out what had happened to his elder brother to reduce him to this state.

Latham listened to his brother's broken voice as he related the story of how he'd lost his right arm, blown off by a stranger he'd never met before.

And all because he was trying to kiss a Mexican!

Larry had got very close to dying through loss of blood, but he was lucky. At the corner of the alleyway he saw a sign saying SURGERY. The old doc inside fought hard and long to save his life. He managed to stop the bleeding and after two weeks of constant care, Larry recovered. Physically, at least.

Mentally, his head was filled with anger, hatred and revenge.

It took three months for Larry to be fit enough to leave. The old doc wouldn't accept a penny in payment, saying he learned more in this one case than in a lifetime of delivering babies and digging out bullets.

No one witnessed the shooting. No one knew who the stranger was or indeed, who the Mexican girl was. The only clue Larry had was that he heard the name Maria. At least, he thought he did.

As he lay on the ground, shock having set in at seeing his shattered arm lying beside him, he either heard the name, or imagined it. Either way, the name Maria in Mexico was as common as flies on a steer. But it was all he had.

Now it was all Latham had. At the end of three weeks, his brother died peacefully in his sleep.

And Latham vowed to dedicate the rest of his life to get even with the man who had caused this.

9

Doc Mayweather was a very persuasive man.

The mayor wanted to form a committee, of course, to discuss the situation. 'We have to be democratic,' he'd argued.

'You can be as democratic as you like lying in your grave,' the doc answered. 'There's already been six killed, and I believe Mitch Evans is right in his summation. You've seen the note from Maria, you want to see the bodies those two boys brought into town?'

'No, no, of course not,' the mayor replied.

'Then let's get some men together. We let Parry get away with this and this town is as good as doomed.' Doc waited for the mayor's response.

The mayor was sweating profusely; he reached into his jacket pocket and brought out a handkerchief. Taking his derby off, he mopped his brow.

He replaced his derby, put the hand-kerchief back in his pocket, and coughed.

'Well, seeing as how you put it that way —'

'We don't have time to dillydally, Mr Mayor,' the doc added.

'OK, let's do this!' The words were firm even if the delivery was not.

Mitch was astonished when, some fifteen minutes after the doc had left, he returned with a motley selection of some twenty men. All were armed, one with a flintlock that looked as if it had never been fired.

'We got two choices,' Mitch said. 'We ride out to the Bar JWM, and possibly meet up with Latham Parry and his cronies, or we wait here till they ride in. Cos sure as eggs is eggs, Parry ain't gonna let this go.'

'I reckon town is a better option,' Doc Mayweather suggested. 'Parry won't be expecting a welcoming committee; we'll have an element of surprise.'

'I agree,' Mitch said. 'I figure Parry is after me and the doc, here. He's already killed my brother and his family, and Maria sent a note to the doc, so it seems likely.'

'Parry doesn't know about the note, does he?' the mayor asked.

'He doesn't know what the note said,' Mitch replied, 'but he knows there is one. Seems to me he's planning to get rid of the surrounding ranches and take over the Bar JWM, unless we stop him here and now.'

There was no further argument, so Mitch spoke again.

'I reckon Parry will make the surgery his target. We need a couple of men opposite, up on the roof. I want half of you men to spread out along the street, keeping well down and giving yourselves a clear shot to the front of the surgery.

'The rest of you do the same at the rear. Parry is no fool, he won't ride in gung-ho. Me, the doc and Cal will be inside the surgery, so make sure your shots don't hit us, OK?'

Two of the younger men elected for the roof opposite; the rest, most aged over fifty: shopkeepers, a barber, and the liveryman, formed two groups and took up positions at the front and rear of the surgery.

The streets were deserted; even the saloon closed and locked its doors. The whole town was eerily silent.

Now they waited.

Parry called a halt as they neared the scene of frantic buzzards fighting over two carcasses in the dying rays of the sun.

'Goddamnit,' Parry muttered under his breath as he recognized one of the horses, still ground-hitched.

He wasn't in the slightest bit bothered about the loss of another two men; in fact he was angry that they, too, had failed to stop the buckboard getting to Calvary.

His crew had different thoughts. Four of their men had now been killed. Were they chasing a gunny? They all knew Cal, and he was no shootist. They'd already heard of Clancy's death, they'd left

Haystack back on the trail, more dead than alive, and now Jones and Wilmington — or what was left of them — lay dead in the dirt.

Burning down the Evans place had been bad enough, but now it looked like they were being led into a gunfight.

They were cowhands, not gunfighters.

'We better get these two buried, boss,' one of the men said.

'We ain't got time and I ain't got the inclination. We ride on,' Parry growled. 'You can take care of 'em on the way back,' he added. 'Now, let's ride.'

The red mist that had filled Latham Parry's eyes was fading away as his scheming brain began to function once more.

Reaching a crest in the trail, Parry called a halt. From here, he could look down into the valley where Calvary nestled peacefully amid a fertile plain.

The sun had disappeared behind the western horizon and, although it would be a full moon, for now the moon was clouded out. Parry took his old army field glasses out and focused on the twinkling lights that shone on Main Street, Calvary.

Parry was no fool. He felt like riding into town, guns blazing, but caution prevailed.

Evans's brother and that scumbag Cal Morgan must have made it to town and, given that Morgan knew Haystack and the two line riders, surely they'd put two and two together.

Parry vowed that, come hell or high water, Cal Morgan would be the first to die.

Something wasn't right down there, Parry thought as he scanned the town. It was quiet — too quiet. The only lights showing were the street ones. Every building was shrouded in darkness.

'They know we're comin',' Parry said to no one in particular.

'What's the plan, boss?' one of the men asked.

Parry was unsure of the next step. He'd been hoping to have the element of surprise on his side, but now that possibility had evaporated. He thought for a few moments, then said,

'We split up. I'll ride in from the west, you four men from the east. But keep your eyes wide open. I figure they'll be in the surgery. Douse some o' them streetlights as you pass.'

'What then?' another asked.

'Get them arrows ready; we'll smoke 'em out. Be careful, though. They might have men posted out on Main.'

'Hell, boss, that could mean a shoot-out!'

'So?'

'So, none of us is a shootist. We signed on as cowhands, not killers.'

'Bit late for that, now,' Parry said with a smile that didn't reach his eyes. 'You wanna ride out? Go ahead.'

'Hell, boss, I ain't no quitter,' the man said quickly. He knew that if he tried to leave, Parry would backshoot him for sure.

'You boys will be well rewarded when this is all over; we'll have the Bar JWM and the Bar-B,' Parry said, and there was a wistful look in his eyes.

None of the men asked any more questions or made any comments, but they all thought, *Yeah, if we survive.*

Now that his most trusted right-hand man had gone, Parry had no yardstick for the motley crew he was saddled with. He knew that the man who had spoken out was telling the truth: they weren't shootists, but then, neither were the townsfolk of Calvary.

Doc Mayweather was becoming increasingly concerned about his old friend, Josh Winters.

The note he had received from Maria had been pretty explicit; Josh's health was failing fast and he knew he needed to get out there to see him as quickly as possible. He knew Maria well, and she was not the sort of woman who would panic.

'Mitch, I have to get out to the Bar JWM,' the doc said in a hushed voice.

Mitch didn't reply straight away. He rubbed his chin, then said, 'Could be signing your own death warrant, Doc.'

'I know, but I reckon if Parry and his men are heading here, they'll use the main trail from the ranch. They think they have nothing to fear, whereas I can ride overland and, in the dark, they won't even get a glimpse of me.' Mayweather waited for Mitch's response.

Mitch was silent, thinking.

'Son, I was born and raised in Calvary, I know this territory like the back of my hand. I ain't a gunman, so my use here is minimal — 'cept doctorin' — and Agnes will be here for that. She's more than just my housekeeper.' Again Mayweather waited.

'You sure about this, Doc?' Mitch asked.

'I've known Josh Winters for nigh on forty years; anything I can do to help him, then by heaven, I'll do it.'

Mitch could tell that Doc Mayweather had made his mind up and that argument was futile.

'You go careful, Doc. You got a gun?'

'Sure. I ain't stupid.' The doc smiled

and grabbed his bag. 'My horse is out back. I'll leave town by one of the alleyways. I could make the trip blindfolded.' Again he gave a reassuring smile.

The two men shook hands and Doc Mayweather left by the back door.

The doc had been right about Agnes. She knew what the doc would do even before he did.

She had the doc's horse saddled and hitched to the back fence. She'd also checked the Winchester and made sure it was fully loaded.

'Agnes, what would I do without you?'

'You'd never find your breeches, that's for sure,' Agnes answered. She was trying hard not to show her concern. 'You take care out there, Doc,' was all she said.

'You can be sure of it. I'll be back before you know it.' The doc smiled and mounted up. With a last smile, he waved and set off for the Bar JWM.

Latham Parry looked at the men who sat idly in their saddles. He knew most of them by name, but had confided in none of them. They were just cowhands, necessary for the smooth running of the ranch.

Some were smoking and chatting, others slaking their thirst with the tepid water in their canteens. His gaze rested on one man.

He was younger than the rest of the crew and Parry didn't recognize him at all. He watched as the man lifted out his rifle from the saddle scabbard and checked the load, then replaced it. He then took out his handgun and checked the load in that as well.

'You,' Parry called out. 'I don't reckon I seen you before.'

The man calmly walked his horse closer to Parry. 'Name's Moran, Silas Moran but most folks call me Si.'

'How long you been at the Bar JWM?' Parry asked. There was something about this man — boy really: he looked no more than eighteen or nineteen.

'Includin' today?'

'Includin' today,' Parry said.

'Three days, boss. Man called Clancy hired me.'

'Didn't say nothin' to me about any hirin',' Parry said.

The boy just shrugged.

Parry studied the boy. His clean-shaven face didn't look as if he could even grow a beard and his dark-blue eyes looked at Parry unblinking. His build was slight but his jaw was set firm, his face expressionless.

'You ever been to Calvary?' Parry asked.

'Nope, I was riding through your east range, didn't know I was trespassin', when I was stopped by the man called Clancy.'

'What made him hire you?' Parry asked.

Again, Si just shrugged. 'Asked me if I was looking for work and had I ever worked with cattle, then offered me a job.'

Parry's brain was working overtime. He formulated a new plan.

'Well, I got a job for you. No one knows you in Calvary so you'll make an ideal spy. I want to know exactly where Brad Evans's brother is, as well as that rat Cal Morgan. Reckon you can do that?'

'Sure,' Si answered.

'And find out how many men, if any, he's got lined up.'

'You figure they're waitin' on us?'

'There ain't no movement down there that I could see. The town's too quiet.' Parry took out his pocket watch and flipped the lid open. 'It's a quarter after six, town's usually busy. There's no one on the street. So, yes, I figure they're waitin' on us.'

'OK. I'll be back as soon as I can,' Si said. Without another word he wheeled his mount round and rode off to Calvary.

Twenty minutes later Si reined in at the edge of town. He took out his makings and rolled a cigarette; igniting the lucifer with his thumb, he lit up and drew deeply.

It took another five minutes for Si to finish the cigarette and in that time he saw not a soul. He could see the buckboard, horseless, parked on the side of

131

Main Street, and a light shone from the saloon on the opposite side of the street.

He tossed the butt to the ground and walked his horse slowly towards the saloon: as good a place as any to start, he thought. Eyes and ears alert for any sound or movement, Si dismounted and hitched his pony to the rail. He took off his Stetson and banged the dust from his clothes as best he could, replaced his hat, adjusted his gunbelt and mounted the three steps to the boardwalk.

He paused on the boardwalk and looked down Main Street: first to the left, then to the right.

Nothing. No sound, no movement. Nothing.

He looked over the batwings and into the saloon. Lights were burning, three or four oil lamps were hanging on hooks fixed to the wall and in the centre of the low ceiling hung an overly ornate chandelier, its glass baubles sparkling in the light from a dozen or so candles.

The wooden tables and chairs were cheap and arranged haphazardly, as if

132

no one really cared. Glasses had been left on the tables, along with a few cheap ashtrays, all overflowing. There were several paintings on the walls, stained by tobacco smoke. A few landscapes and several of painted ladies in various poses, they were meant to excite the customers, but to Si they looked ridiculous.

There was a long wooden bar running down the right-hand side of the saloon and a brass footrest broken by four none too clean spittoons. The floor was carelessly covered with well-used sawdust and didn't look as if it had been cleaned in weeks.

There were no customers.

There was no one behind the bar either, the place was totally empty.

The place looked and felt like a ghost town.

Si pushed open the batwings and stepped inside. Underfoot, glass crunched and the floorboards creaked. His hand rested on the butt of his Colt — just in case.

He walked to the bar and peered over

it. The trapdoor was open and a black hole gaped, looking like a portal to hell.

On the wall behind the bar were shelves holding glasses and a couple of dozen bottles, mostly cheap rotgut. A stained mirror was the centrepiece and on it, in gold lettering it said: The Palace Saloon.

Si walked behind the bar-top and grabbed a bottle and a shot glass, then he walked to the rear of the saloon, pulled out a chair and sat, his back to the wall, facing the batwings.

He poured himself a shot and downed it in one, then refilled the glass and waited.

Thomas O'Malley, proprietor, barman and general dogsbody of the Palace Saloon, stepped outside the surgery to get some fresh air, rested his Winchester against the wall and took out his makings.

O'Malley was in his later fifties, portly rather than fat. He was a large Irishman who'd come to America in his youth. After the untimely death of his parents, he left New York and travelled West, never making it past Calvary.

134

He started working in the Palace as a swampy and glass collector, before becoming barman. The then owner, Walt Fisher, was in his seventies, and not a well man. On his deathbed, in front of witnesses, he left the Palace to Thomas, and for the past twenty-five years Thomas O'Malley had been a contented man.

His one regret was that he'd never married.

Sighing inwardly, he took out a paper and opened his tobacco pouch.

It was then he saw the horse hitched outside his saloon.

He forgot about making a cigarette, grabbed his rifle and went to get Mitch.

'Mitch, Mitch! There's a stranger in town.'

'OK, OK! Calm down. Where is he?' Mitch asked, keeping his voice low.

'There's a horse hitched outside my saloon.'

'How'd you know it's a stranger?' Mitch asked.

'Who else could it be?' Thomas said with a straight face.

Mitch almost laughed, but held it in check. 'I'll go over and see who it is.'

'Hang on, Mitch. I'll come with you,' Cal said. 'You're a stranger here too, so everyone'll be a stranger to you.'

Mitch did laugh this time.

Cal grabbed his crutch and both men, after checking their guns for the umpteenth time, left the surgery.

'You recognize the horse?' Mitch asked.

'It ain't a Bar JWM horse, that's for sure,' Cal replied. 'Never seen him before.'

'That don't mean he ain't from the Bar JWM,' Mitch replied.

They reached the saloon. Mitch put a hand up and laid a finger to his lips. Silently, he moved to one of the windows and took a look inside.

'There's a fella in the far corner,' Mitch whispered. 'Take a looksee.'

Cal peered through the window at the stranger seated quite calmly with a bottle in front of him.

'Recognize him?'

'No,' Cal replied. 'At least, I never seen him out at the Bar JWM.'

'OK, let's go in. Keep your gun hand close,' Mitch said.

He pushed through the batwings and both men entered the saloon.

'Beginning to think this was a ghost town,' the stranger said. 'Grab a glass, be good to have some company.'

'Thank you kindly,' Mitch said and grabbed two shot glasses.

'Name's Silas Moran,' said the stranger, passing the bottle.

'Mitch Evans, and this here's my pard, Cal Morgan.'

There was an almost imperceptible change in Si's expression, but Mitch saw it.

'Cal Morgan?' Si said.

'You heard the name before?' Mitch asked.

'No, just making sure I heard you right,' Si replied.

Mitch knew he was lying. 'You passing through or looking for work?'

'Work. You know of any?'

'Not around here. There's trouble brewing. Guess you made a wrong call stopping here tonight.' Mitch eyed the younger man carefully, looking for any change, however small.

Si casually picked his shot glass up and drained the contents. 'Guess I'll be moving on, then. Lubbock far?'

'Four, maybe five hours' ride,' Cal answered.

'Anywhere I can get some grub?' Si asked.

'Not tonight,' Mitch answered. 'If'n I was you, I'd hit the trail.'

'That a threat?'

'No, that's advice,' Mitch said and drained his glass. 'Thanks for the drink. You can leave the money — and the bottle — on the bar-top.'

'Reckon I'll keep the bottle. Town sure ain't a friendly place,' Si said.

'Ain't a good night for 'friendly',' Mitch replied and stood, followed by Cal.

Mitch walked towards the batwings, followed by Cal; then he stopped and beckoned Cal ahead. He had a funny feeling running through his belly. He waited and as Cal passed him, whispered, 'Get ready!'

Cal looked puzzled, but said nothing.

It was then that Mitch heard the sounds he had expected, the scraping of a chair on the rough wooden floorboards and the metallic click of a hammer being pulled back.

What followed seemed to be acted out in slow motion. In one fluid movement, Mitch pushed Cal to the floor and drew his Colt.

Two shots rang out almost simultaneously. One thudded into the wall, harmlessly. The other found its target.

10

Doc Mayweather made good time getting out to the Bar JWM.

He reined in on a low rise and looked down into the compound surrounding the house, barns and corral.

It was eerily quiet and the only light that shone came from the ranch house. Slowly, Doc Mayweather walked his horse down the slope and on to the main trail and headed towards the house.

When he was fifty yards from the front porch steps Mayweather stopped, dismounted and grabbed his black bag.

He led his mount to the water trough, then headed for the house, his ears ringing in the silence.

As he mounted the porch steps a voice from inside called out, 'Who's there?'

'Maria? It's me, Doc Mayweather. I got your note.'

The sound of the key turning in the

large lock and the sliding back of bolts sounded unnaturally loud in the still of the night. Eventually, the door swung open revealing Maria.

'Thank God,' she said and ushered the doc inside. She quickly relocked and bolted the front door.

'Perhaps I should see Josh first. I have many questions to ask,' Mayweather said.

'Yes, yes, of course.' Maria led the way up to Josh's bedroom.

The room was in darkness and the air carried the scent of death. Mayweather opened the curtains and Maria lit a lantern.

Josh Winters's breathing was shallow and laboured. Mayweather felt for a pulse, then gave a deep sigh.

'The end is near, Maria,' he said in a strained voice. 'There's little I can do for him.'

Maria nodded. She knew in her heart of hearts that Josh was dying.

'What will you do when ...?' Mayweather asked.

'I'll stay here,' Maria answered with

iron determination in her voice.

'But won't the ranch have to be sold? I mean, Josh has no relatives.'

'He left the ranch to me. The papers are with a lawyer in Lubbock.'

'Amos?' Mayweather asked.

'Yes.'

'Well I'll be,' Mayweather said. 'You're gonna need all the help you can get to both run this place and control Latham Parry.'

'Mr Parry will not be working here for much longer,' Maria stated.

'With luck you might not see him again after today,' Mayweather said.

'Do you know what's going on?' Maria asked.

Doc Mayweather shook his head. 'Not all of it.' He went on to tell Maria the little he did know. Maria's face went from shock to horror.

'None of this was done with Josh's knowledge!' Maria said firmly.

'No one thinks it was. Brad Evans's brother is in town, along with Cal Morgan and some of the townsfolk.

They're expecting Parry and his men at any moment, if he hasn't already arrived.' Doc Mayweather took out his pocket watch and checked the time.

Before they could continue their conversation they both looked towards the large bed. Josh, eyes wide open, was trying to say something.

Maria rushed to his side and leant down close to him. But Josh beckoned his old friend close, too.

His voice was weak, and punctuated with gasps for breath as he tried to delay death for as long as possible.

'Look — after — Maria. See — Amos.'

He broke off as a coughing fit took over.

'Don't try to speak,' Maria said. 'Rest, my love.'

Josh's eyes sparkled briefly as he heard her words — especially the last two. He face broke into a creased smile, he squeezed her hand once, then his grip went limp and his eyes closed.

Josh Winters died with the image of Maria's face the last thing he saw.

Mitch Evans and Si Moran stood facing each other, their handguns still smoking and the smell of black powder wafting through the Palace Saloon. A stony silence, made deafening by the explosions of two Colts seconds earlier, filled the saloon. Cal, still lying on the floor, stared open-mouthed, wondering why no more shots had been fired. Then it became obvious.

The barrel of Si Moran's pistol drooped downwards, then fell to the floor. Moran's head sagged as he looked at the rapidly spreading blood that gushed from his chest. Then Moran's legs buckled and he collapsed, face down on the sawdust-covered floor. The expression on his face was one of surprise more than pain and, as he fell, his eyes never left the face of Mitch Evans, as if he were expecting him to fall dead as well.

'Goddamn!' Cal managed to utter. 'You knew he was gonna do that?'

'Kinda,' Mitch replied. He holstered his gun. 'You OK?'

144

'Yeah, I'm fine, thanks to you,' Cal replied. 'You reckon he's one of Parry's men?'

'He was. Something about him I jus' didn't take a likin' to. Let's get back to the doc's place. Parry won't wait much longer.'

'You hear that, boss?'

''Course I heard it, I ain't deaf,' Parry almost spat out. 'Seems that kid, what was his name?'

'Si, boss, Si Moran.'

'Seems he reckoned on his gunplay. Couldn't tell if'n it was one shot or two,' Parry said, mainly to himself.

'What do we do now, boss?' another of his men asked.

'We ride, boys. We ride in and burn the hell outa that surgery and everyone in it!' Parry's voice began to rise and there was a glint of madness in his eyes as he spoke that didn't go unnoticed by his men.

Parry didn't even notice the looks that passed between his gang, so engrossed was he in his hatred of Morgan who, as

145

far as he was concerned, had betrayed him. None of this would have happened if Morgan had done his job. Now he had Brad Evans's brother to contend with as well.

'Boss.' A tall rangy man, known as Cutter — no one knew his real name, and he never let on — spoke for the first time. 'Seems to me we got ourselves a situation here.'

'No shit,' Parry growled.

Cutter was not put off. Of all the men on the Bar JWM, he was not afraid of Parry. An ex-army sergeant with a mean streak, he always carried two Bowie knives: one in a sheath attached to the rear of his belt; the other inside his left boot. Cutter was a loner, kept pretty much to himself. He did his job and no more.

'Sure, we can ride hell for leather into Calvary and maybe we can shoot up the town, burn the surgery down — and maybe the whole town. On the other hand, we know they're waiting for us. We got no surprise element left. We can ride into Calvary and sure as I'm sitting here we'll get cut down like dogs.

'You want the Bar JWM? Well, it's just sitting there with an old man and a woman, maybe cookie and a couple of the older hands. They gonna put up a fight? Makes sense to me: we ride back to the ranch and wait for them to attack us and we do the cutting down.'

Cutter rolled himself a cigarette, lit it and drew deeply. Parry sat, staring at Cutter, his brain working overtime.

The rest of the men sat atop their mounts, furtively glancing at each other and desperately trying not to catch the eye of Parry.

Parry didn't want to back down on his own plan, but what the man Cutter said made sense. He'd have control of the Bar JWM and they'd have the advantage over Morgan and Evans.

Suddenly, Parry smiled, or at least as close to a smile as he ever got.

'I like it,' was all he said.

There was a palpable sigh of relief from the men. At least they wouldn't die today.

'Where the hell are they?' Thomas O'Malley was sweating heavily and the tension was getting to him.

His question was answered by a knock on the front door.

'Who's there?' O'Malley shouted.

'It's me and Mitch,' Cal answered. 'Open up!'

O'Malley released the bolts and unlocked the door. 'What was the shooting about?' O'Malley asked. 'You two OK?'

'Yeah, we're fine,' Cal said. 'Seems Parry sent a newcomer into town and he figured on making a name for hisself.' Cal smiled. 'Mitch here shot him down, saved my bacon, too.'

Mitch, who had not uttered a word since returning, took off his hat and helped himself to a coffee.

'You been mighty quiet, Mitch,' Cal said, also grabbing a coffee.

'Thinking, is all,' Mitch answered absently.

'Wanna share those thoughts?' Cal asked.

'I was thinking, if Parry and his men were on the outskirts of town, he would have heard those shots,' Mitch said.

'So?'

'So, if it was me, I'd know for sure that I was riding into an ambush.' Mitch sipped his coffee and waited for any comments.

When none were forthcoming, Mitch said to O'Malley, 'How often do you hear gunfire in Calvary?'

'Hell, the last time was over two, maybe three months ago, and that was a drunk who fell over and shot his own foot,' O'Malley said, laughing.

'My point exactly,' Mitch said. 'What's the most vulnerable place right now? Here in town, or the Bar JWM?'

'Hell, you reckon they're gonna make a move on ol' Josh?' Cal said.

'That's what I would do. You read that note from Maria. The trail drive set off two days ago so, as far as we know, there's only her, Doc Mayweather and maybe one or two hands out there.'

Mitch watched the faces of the men

in the room before adding: 'I don't think they're coming into town.'

'We have to leave here, Maria,' Doc Mayweather said.

'Why? The house is secure. Josh made sure of that,' Maria said.

'No house is totally secure. We need to get Josh out and you off to Lubbock. If Parry gets back here with his men it'll be for a showdown. He won't know about Josh.'

Maria nodded slowly.

'Make sure you get the will, and keep it safe. I'm sure Amos will have a copy, too. Then we can make it legal and above board and, tomorrow, arrange for Josh's funeral.' The doc wiped his brow and checked his watch again.

'I'll get a buggy sorted,' the doc went on.

'No. I'll do it, I know where things are. But first let's get Josh downstairs.' Maria went to the bed and drew the single sheet over Josh's body. 'Can you manage to lift him?' she asked.

'Of course,' Mayweather answered, and between them they managed to get the body down into the hall.

'There's some cord in the kitchen,' Maria said. 'If you can secure the ... the ... sheet, I'll hitch up the buggy.' With that she unlocked the front door and made her way to the barn.

By the time Maria had hitched up the pony and driven it to the house, Doc Mayweather had trussed up the body of Josh Winters and dragged it out on to the porch. Between them they loaded the corpse on to the buggy.

'Shouldn't take us more than three hours to get to Lubbock,' Mayweather said, as he hauled himself up into the driver's seat.

Maria had a sudden thought. 'Do you think we should leave a note?'

'Definitely not! Hell — 'scuse my language, Maria. If it comes to a gunfight in town and Parry wins, it'll be him that finds any note and he'll come after you.'

'But ... I guess you are right,' Maria answered.

'Let's get to Lubbock, at least the night will be to our advantage.' With that, Mayweather released the brake, flicked the long-handled whip and they set off.

Having finished washing the few dishes from the evening meal, Beefsteak was making his way back to the cookhouse, looking forward to a slug of whiskey from his secret stash.

He saw Maria drive the buggy out of the barn and watched as Doc Mayweather dragged what looked like a body from the front door of the ranch house.

All thoughts of whiskey disappeared as he stared open-mouthed at the scene. He stood transfixed, undecided as to what to do.

Was Josh dead?

By the time he came to his senses Maria and Mayweather had loaded the body on to the buggy and set off, heading north.

He dropped the dishes and shouted out, but they obviously didn't hear him. 'What the hell?' he mouthed.

Beefsteak ran to the bunkhouse; there were only four hands on the ranch, the rest on the drive, except for …

He burst through the bunkhouse door, causing the four men inside, idly playing cards, to jump up in surprise.

'Something's goin' down here, an' I don't like it,' Beefsteak yelled.

'What the hell you on about?' one of the hands asked.

'I jus' seen that doc and Maria load a body on to a buggy and hightail it north,' Beefsteak said breathlessly. 'Don't you think it strange that Parry and his cronies have disappeared and the rest of the boys are out on the drive? There's only us five here.'

'There's Maria and Josh,' another man piped up.

'Are you deaf or jus' plain stupid? I jus' tol' you, I seed them head out north. There's only us here.'

'So what you think is goin' down?'

'I figure Parry is making his move on the Bar JWM, that's what I think,' Beefsteak said. 'You boys better get your rifles — and make sure they're loaded!'

It took Parry and his men forty minutes to get back to the Bar JWM. He called a halt on the rise that led down to the ranch house and outbuildings.

'OK. We split up. I want four men to the rear of the ranch house, the rest with me at the front. We'll go on foot from here. There might be one or two hands around, they'll need to be taken care of.'

'Even the cook?' one man asked.

''Specially the cook,' Parry said. 'He's been here years and worships the ground old man Winters walks on.'

'Now make sure the back is covered, I don't want anyone to leave that house. Got it? I'll give you ten minutes to get in position.'

The men nodded.

'Check your weapons and be alert,' Parry said, then added, 'I don't want any shootin' till you see my signal. I'll shoot a flaming arrow so's you can see it.'

The men grunted acknowledgement

and made their way in the dark towards the rear of the ranch house.

Dark clouds scudded across the sky, obliterating the moon's pale blue light before moving on, allowing the moon to paint the landscape once more.

In that moment of almost utter darkness, Parry suddenly had an odd feeling. Something wasn't right, but he couldn't put his finger on it.

He peered through the gloom at the ranch house. It was shrouded in darkness, but that was nothing unusual: Parry knew old man Winters was no night bird.

Then he realized what was wrong.

There were no lights in the bunkhouse.

'You want me to signal, boss?'

'No. Hold fire. Something ain't right down there. I reckon there's no more'n five hands down there, so why is there no light showing in the bunkhouse?'

'Maybe they's sleeping,' one man said.

'Too early for that. No, I reckon they know something's goin' down,' Parry said, more to himself than anyone else.

At that moment shots rang out. It was

impossible to tell where they came from, but Parry knew he had been right in his assessment of the situation.

'Spread out and keep low, them critters is protecting Winters.'

At the rear of the ranch house a full-scale shooting war was going on, but in the darkness, with only muzzle flashes to aim at, it was almost impossible to hit a target.

Almost, but not, as it proved, impossible. A lucky shot from Beefsteak found its target and a high-pitched scream rent the air.

'Dex, you OK?' a voice called in the darkness.

'No, I ain't OK, I bin hit,' Dex replied.

'Shit! I didn't sign on for none o' this crap. I didn't figure on burning out the Bar-B, either.' The voice belonged to Jim Brawn, a cowhand who, with the promise of extra money, had agreed to be one of Parry's inner circle.

'You hit bad, Dex?'

'My shoulder. Sure stings a tad,' came the reply.

'Let's get the hell outa here,' Jim said.

'With you there, pard.'

Slowly and carefully the two men began to crawl to the side of the ranch house furthest away from their attackers.

Having rounded the side of the house the two men relaxed.

'Let me take a look at your shoulder,' Jim said, and got to his knees.

That was his first and last mistake.

Sighting down the long barrel of his Winchester, Latham Parry took careful aim and squeezed the trigger.

He couldn't see the man he was about to kill, but was sure it was one of the ranch hands defending the Bar JWM.

The slug hit Jim high in the chest, just below his neck and exploded out through his shoulder blades, bringing with it a cascade of blood and bone. The force of the bullet flung Jim backwards, landing heavily in the soft sand.

He didn't move again.

Dex, despite his wound, rushed to his partner's side. That was his mistake.

Again, Parry held his breath and gently

squeezed the trigger of his rifle.

Dex soundlessly slumped forwards and landed on top of his already dead partner.

Parry smiled to himself, completely unaware he'd just killed two of his own men.

11

There was a knock at the door. Instantly Mitch Evans drew his sidearm.

Placing a finger to his lips to quieten the men, he approached the front door of the doc's surgery.

Cautiously, he opened the door, his gun pointing at the visitor.

Ellie-Rae O'Hara gasped, almost dropping the tray she was holding.

'Miss O'Hara — Ellie.' Mitch almost whispered the words.

'I didn't expect to be greeted with a gun.' Her look was fierce, but her voice faltered.

'I'm sorry,' Mitch said, reholstering his weapon. 'For a second we, that is to say, I —'

'I brought some eggs, bacon and fresh-baked bread; figured you boys might be hungry,' Ellie interrupted. She pulled off the cloth that covered the tray, revealing steaming-hot food. The smell had Mitch's juices running as he realized he hadn't eaten since breakfast.

Stepping aside he said, 'Sorry. Please, come in.'

'No, I won't come in, just take the tray,' Ellie said.

The disappointment on Mitch's face was all too obvious.

'What are you planning to do?' she asked.

Mitch explained the situation, finishing up by telling her he was going out to the Bar JWM as he was sure Latham Parry was headed back there.

There was a hint of fear in Ellie's eyes. 'You be careful, Mitch,' she said. 'I'd hate not to see you again.'

As Mitch took the tray, her hand gently brushed his. 'I'd sure hate not to see you again, Ellie,' he said.

Ellie smiled, turned and left. Mitch watched her as she crossed the street, willing her to look back just once. To his utter delight she did, the smile still on her face, and Mitch smiled right back before she disappeared from his view.

Mitch calmed himself down, closed the door and went into the back room; the aroma of the bacon filled the room.

'Dig in, boys,' he said, placing the tray on the table.

It took no longer than ten minutes to devour the food.

Sipping on hot coffee, Mitch addressed the assembled men. 'I'm riding out to the Bar JWM —' he began.

Cal quickly interrupted. 'I'm riding with you.'

'No!' Mitch's answer was emphatic. 'I will do this alone. I have the darkness and surprise on my side and this is my fight.'

The men were silent for a while. It was Cal who voiced his objection.

'You need someone to cover your back,' he said.

'That's the last thing I need,' Mitch said. 'You men aren't experienced and I want no more killing — except for one man: Latham Parry!

'Keep alert, just in case they do decide

to come here. Keep your ears and eyes open. If I'm not back by noon, you'll know I failed. OK?'

'I don't like it,' Cal said.

'Whether you like it or not,' Mitch said, 'that's the way it's going to be.'

Mitch then turned to Brett Larson, manager of the Palace Saloon. 'You need to send a man to Midland and tell the sheriff there what's going down here. We need to get the law involved.'

'Leave it to me,' Brett said and left the surgery.

As Doc Mayweather crested a rise in the trail he saw the lights of Lubbock flickering in the distance.

Without being too obvious, the doc had been keeping an eye out on the trail behind them. It was too dark to see anything definitive, but he was sure they weren't being followed. The darkness, he figured, was both an ally and a hindrance. If he could see nothing, then, if there was someone following, they wouldn't be able to see either.

'Should be there in about an hour,' the doc said.

'It's late, I hope we can get a room,' Maria answered.

'No problem there. My old friend Doc Fleetwood will put us up. He'll grumble and moan, but he's got a heart of gold,' Mayweather told her.

Fifty minutes later Mayweather pulled the buggy to a halt outside the home of his friend. He eased his aching bones to the ground, stretched, and walked up the short path to the front door.

It took Fleetwood five minutes to respond, and even Maria, still seated in the buggy, could hear him grumbling as he unlocked the door.

'Who the h —' He stopped when he saw Mayweather. 'In hell you doin' here? Don't you know what time it is?'

'Of course I know what the time is, but this is urgent, we need a room for the night,' Mayweather said.

'We?'

'It's a long story, Mac, that can only be told over a brandy and coffee and one of your fine cigars,' Mayweather replied with a smile. 'But first, sad news, Josh Winters died — natural causes — and we must get the body inside.'

Mac Fleetwood tightened his dressing-gown belt and helped his old friend carry the body inside. Maria, still seated, her back bolt upright, wiped a tear from her eye and waited for Mayweather to return.

The moon broke through dark thunder-clouds and spread an eerie blue light on the Bar JWM ranch.

The shooting had stopped for a while now, and Parry was getting more agitated and frustrated than ever.

He wanted to call out to his men, but was wary of giving his position away. There were still no lights showing in both the ranch house and the bunkhouse and, with all the shooting, surely that Gonzalez woman would have been curious, to say the least.

Parry's brain was working overtime. Why no lights? Why no shooting?

Where the hell were his men?

Impatience was getting the better of him. After cocking the Winchester, Parry began to belly-crawl towards the side of the ranch house where he'd seen the two men he'd shot at. Inch by inch he made his way forwards through the cloying sand, every second expecting a shot to come his way.

None did.

The deathly silence was beginning to get to Parry. Dark clouds scudding across the sky blanked out the moon momentarily before it revealed itself again, casting ghostly shadows that moved like silent wraiths in the cool night air.

It took ten minutes for Parry to reach a position where he could see two un-moving bodies, their faces turned away from him. He slid forwards, a cold sweat covering his body from both the exertion and the tension building in him.

Reaching the first of the bodies, he put the rifle to one side and rolled the man over to face him.

'Shit!' He said the word loudly and

immediately shots came in his direction. He kept low, unable to take his eyes off Dex. The realization that he'd shot his own men dawned on him and in the blink of an eye he answered his own questions.

There were no lights in the ranch house because the ranch house was empty, and although he didn't know for sure, instinctively he knew the other three men had high-tailed it out. The reason for no shooting until now was that he was the only one to shoot at.

Mitch hurriedly finished the food and tried to rid his mind of the image of Ellie-Rae.

He gathered up his Colt, checked the load and holstered it. He did the same with the Winchester.

'How much spare ammo do we have?' Mitch asked.

The mayor, who also ran the town's only store, answered, 'I got a stack of .45s in the store; not much call for 'em.'

'OK, let's get some and then I'm off. Remember, keep your eyes and ears open at all times,' Mitch told them again.

The assembled men nodded in silence. Only Cal voiced his objection.

'It's plumb crazy you goin' alone,' he said. 'You ain't got no idea how many men are with him.'

'It's my fight, Cal,' was all Mitch said as he left the surgery with the mayor. Five minutes later Mitch was fully loaded with ammunition. He mounted up and, without glancing back, rode out of Calvary, heading north to the Bar JWM.

Ellie-Rae watched him leave town. A single tear rolled down her cheek.

At the edge of town, Mitch edged his horse into a gentle canter; it was too dark for a full-out gallop. He knew his animal was sure footed as he travelled along the well-used trail.

He had one thought on his mind, and one thought only: to kill Latham Parry, regardless of his own safety.

When he'd made his decision to travel alone, it was based on the fact that he had no family, no one in his life to live for. Now, as long as he read the unspoken message from Ellie-Rae, he thought there might be a reason to live after all. Suddenly, his mind drifted from Ellie-Rae. He needed to plan carefully on how to surprise the Bar JWM gang, as he now thought of them. Were they gunnies, or just cowhands coerced, maybe, into riding with Parry?

Mitch knew now that he didn't want to die — not if he could help it.

Filled with this new resolve, he decided to approach the ranch from the rear and see if he could make it to the ranch house and speak with Maria.

Then he'd plan what he would do.

His reverie was broken by the silhouette of three riders galloping recklessly towards him.

Mitch immediately turned his horse off the trail; with any luck they wouldn't see him.

But Lady Luck wasn't with him. The three men reined in.

'Where you headin', mister?' one of the men asked.

'What business is that of yourn?' Mitch replied.

'If'n you're headin' fer the Bar JWM I'd turn back if I was you,' the man countered.

'Oh? And why is that?' Mitch asked.

'There's trouble brewin' and we high-tailed it outa there,' the man said.

'Latham Parry,' Mitch said. It was a statement, not a question.

'He a pal of yours?'

'Only if hell freezes over,' Mitch replied. 'I'm looking for him.'

'Yeah, he's there,' the man said.

'How many men with him?' Mitch asked.

'Only three now.'

'Gunnies?'

'Nah. Cowboys, jus' like we are.' The other two men nodded.

A second man spoke up. 'Parry's mad, crazy as a coot.'

'He burn down the Bar-B?' Mitch waited for their answer.

The three men looked at each other, then their heads sank to their chests.

'Ain't somethin' we're too proud of,' one of the men answered.

'We didn't know what he was planning,' another man said sheepishly. 'If'n we did, we would never have gone with him.'

'You were with him?' Mitch said through gritted teeth.

No one answered, but Mitch knew they had been there.

'You saw my brother die and did nothing to stop it?' Mitch said, his anger mounting.

'Mister, Parry and his two henchmen woulda killed us for sure if we hadn't ridden with them. But I tell you this, we none of us fired any arrows at the house. Clancy and Haystack took care o' that, an' they're both dead now.'

Mitch's palm rested menacingly on the pearl handle of his Colt, which the three men didn't miss.

'Get outa this territory,' Mitch hissed. 'I see any of you again and you're dead.'

Without saying another word the three men dug their spurs in and galloped off south.

Mitch watched the three men until they disappeared from view behind a small bluff. In his head, he wanted to shoot the men, but in his heart, he knew he couldn't.

Latham Parry had to think fast. He was no fool. He knew he was outnumbered; what he didn't know was by how many. All he knew was he had to get back to his horse, pronto, and get the hell out of the Bar JWM.

He'd think what to do next when he was clear of the ranch.

As quickly as he could, Parry began to backtrack. His senses were heightened in the darkness, the slightest sound, the slightest movement was amplified, or so it seemed.

Vaguely, he heard voices in front of him. Parry stopped, screwed up his eyes and peered towards the ranch house.

From the side of the building three men appeared, crouched, their rifles at hip height.

Although they were only around 200

yards away Parry couldn't identify the men, and as the moon was behind them, they couldn't see him as he made his way to his horse.

Reaching the animal, he climbed into the saddle, and, as quietly as he could, rode off into the darkness.

His mind was still swirling. Where the hell were Winters and the Gonzalez woman? Maybe Winters had taken a turn for the worse, gone into town to see the doc.

Clearing the ranch, he reined in and set his mind to work.

Thinking logically, Parry realized that Winters and that Gonzalez woman couldn't have gone to Calvary. There was only one trail a buggy could use, and they'd need a buggy, for Winters was too weak to ride a horse.

That being so, he would have seen them on the trail and Parry was certain sure they hadn't passed him or his men. That left only one possibility.

Lubbock!

Parry's lips parted in what passed for a

smile, but it was more of a sadistic snarl.

He wheeled his animal round and set off at a gallop. He doubted he'd catch them on the trail, but he knew that once he reached Lubbock they would be easy prey.

His grand plan was still alive. He knew he would succeed.

In the distance, Mitch could hear gunfire, sporadic gunshots followed by silence. Whatever was going down, he knew it meant he was right in his assumption that Parry had headed back to the ranch.

Maybe Parry was unaware that three of his men had deserted him. Mitch spurred on; whatever the odds were he was determined to kill Parry.

As he passed through the ornate gateway to the Bar JWM, the shooting stopped. The only sound Mitch could hear were the beats of his mount's hoofs as he thundered down the trail.

Mitch reined in sharply, the animal's hoofs skidding to a halt and sending up plumes of smoking dust.

Silence. Not a sound disturbed the night.

In the distance, Mitch could see the ranch house and outlying buildings silhouetted against a sky that was beginning to come alive again. He hadn't realized, or even thought about the time, but it was certainly later than he had imagined.

Dawn would break in ten to fifteen minutes he reckoned, so, to take advantage of the darkness, he needed to act swiftly.

He took his rifle from the saddle scabbard, grabbed hold of the saddle-bag with spare ammo and dismounted. He ground-hitched his horse and set off on foot.

Less than a hundred yards from the ranch house Mitch halted and crouched low. There were no lights showing in either the bunkhouse or the ranch house and the absence of any sound was almost deafening as he strained his senses to pick up the slightest sound or movement.

Suddenly a rapid volley of shots rent the air, and within minutes the smell of cordite hit Mitch's nostrils. The shooting was pretty close by, but he could see no one; he couldn't even see any muzzle flashes.

Then two things happened almost simultaneously. A muzzle flash was followed by the dull thud of a slug hitting the dirt not six inches from Mitch's position.

'Who the hell's doin' the shootin'?' Mitch called out, moving swiftly to his left.

'Who's doin' the askin'?' a voice replied.

'I'm Mitch Evans, brother of the late Brad Evans. I'm looking for Latham Parry.'

'Goddamn!' came the reply. 'This here's Beefsteak, cook here at the Bar JWM.'

Both men stood and faced one another. Beefsteak waved an arm and three men appeared behind him.

'These boys are with me, the rest of the hands are on the drive, 'cept for the ones who sided with Parry. Two of them are dead yonder by the house, an' we sure didn't kill 'em,' Beefsteak said.

Their conversation was broken by a single shot and a scream.

One of the men, Tom Hardy, took the full impact of a slug. He flew forwards and landed face down.

The man had been back-shot.

Immediately, the four remaining men dived to the ground. Another shot rang out, thudding harmlessly into the dirt.

'You get a bead on that shot?' Mitch asked.

'Over yonder, by that pine tree,' Beefsteak said.

'OK, I'll circle to the left, you take the right. Let's flush that bushwhacker out,' Mitch said. 'You men stay here in case he breaks forward.'

Without another word being spoken, both men began to circle towards the large pine by the side of the corral.

A faint glow appeared on the eastern horizon, heralding the start of a new day. As yet, the crimson fingers of light had not reached the Bar JWM, but soon, too soon, the darkness would vanish as the sun rose higher.

The firing had intensified, it was as if the man was beginning to panic: but the shots were wild, alternating between Mitch, Beefsteak and the two men in the centre line.

Mitch was the first to reach a position where he had a clear shot at the shooter.

'Drop your weapon, mister. We got you covered,' Mitch shouted out.

A single shot rang out, but it didn't come from the lonesome pine, it came from behind Mitch and he went down like a stone.

12

Doc Mayweather was the first to wake up. He stretched his aching bones.

Glad as he was to be under cover for the night, the damn sofa was a foot too short and as hard as a rock.

He made his way through to the kitchen and fed the pot-bellied stove. He hunted around for the coffee pot and coffee. He found a pack of Arbuckles and poured some into the pot, then, adding water, he placed the pot on the stove and sat down, sure that he creaked at every move.

'Too damn old for this,' he said out loud.

'Damn right you are.' The voice almost made Mayweather jump out of his skin.

Mayweather turned in his seat to see a scowling Mac Fleetwood wearing nothing but his long johns.

'Get some clothes on, you old fool.

There's a lady stayin' here,' Mayweather grunted.

'She ain't likely to get too excited over this bony ol' frame,' Mac said. He picked up two cups and placed them on the kitchen table.

'You pour,' he added, and sat down.

Mayweather obliged and the two old friends sat in silence for a while.

'You gonna tell me what in hell's goin' on, Lou?' Mac eventually said.

Doc Mayweather then told Mac everything he knew.

'Shame 'bout ol' Josh. He was a good man,' Mac said. He finished his coffee and stood. 'Right, I'll go see the undertaker and get the funeral arranged. You best get over to see Amos, then we'll all go see the sheriff,' he told Mayweather, then he left the kitchen to get dressed.

Inwardly, Doc Mayweather breathed a sigh of relief. Things would soon be sorted out and Maria would be safe.

His relief was short-lived.

Latham Parry reined in on the outskirts

of Lubbock. The sun was clear of the horizon and already townsfolk were on the street, mainly shopkeepers eager to begin the day's trade.

Parry grabbed his canteen and took a mouthful, swilling it round before spitting it out along with the accumulated dust and grit he'd sucked in during his wild and, sometimes, reckless ride.

He swallowed two mouthfuls, then dismounted. He took off his Stetson, emptied the canteen into it and let his horse drink.

There was a wild look in his eye. All he could think of was killing Winters and that Gonzalez woman.

His contorted features expressed nothing but hate.

Mitch slowly regained consciousness.

He opened his eyes but his vision was blurred. His head throbbed like war drums beating in his temple.

He shook his head, but that made the throbbing worse.

In the distance, he heard the sound

of rifle fire and that brought him to his senses. Now he knew where he was and what he was doing.

His vision was clearing, but only slightly. He could make out the blurred image of the lone pine tree as fingers of deep red spread across the landscape.

Had he been up all night? How long had he been unconscious?

He could answer neither question. Then a name sprang into his head.

Parry! Latham Parry.

In an instant, Mitch was wide awake. His vision cleared and his senses returned. Maybe not totally, but enough.

Rolling on to his stomach, he grabbed his Winchester and sighted down the long barrel.

The light was increasing by the minute and the tree was clearly silhouetted against the rising sun in the east.

Mitch waited.

He knew that sooner or later, the man — or men — secreted behind that tree would show themselves, and when they did …

181

The minutes dragged on. Mitch was comforted by the fact that no shots had come his way; whoever was behind that tree obviously thought he was out of the game, and that was to his advantage.

The firing was sporadic now, each side not wasting shots but waiting for a target.

Mitch held his rifle firmly. His left eye closed as he stared down the sight, breathing evenly, his finger gently resting on the trigger and the butt placed firmly in the crook of his right shoulder. He waited.

His patience was rewarded when one of the men came into view. Mitch didn't hesitate. He squeezed the trigger.

Everything seemed to go in slow motion. Mitch was sure he could see the bullet leave the rifle and speed towards the man in the open: it left a silver trail — real or imaginary — as it travelled forward.

Mitch could almost see the look of surprise on the man's face as the bullet tore into his belly. The man flew backwards, his rifle going one way and he the other; the man landed in a crumpled heap.

Mitch cocked the rifle and again he waited.

But no further shooting was necessary.

A cry rang out from behind the pine tree and a rifle sailed through the air as the voice shouted out, 'Hold your fire, I'm coming out, I'm coming out.'

A man appeared, arms raised high in the air. 'Don't shoot, I'm unarmed, I give up.'

Mitch released his grip on the rifle. The adrenaline that had coursed through his body evaporated as he tried to stand up. His head was in a spin and dizziness almost overcame him, but he struggled to his feet, swaying slightly until he got his balance.

Mitch kept the rifle level at hip height; he was taking no chances as he walked towards the man he hoped was Latham Parry.

Out of the corner of his eye, he caught a glimpse of two men approaching from the far side. Despite the pain he was in,

Mitch smiled to himself. At least the men who had ridden with him were OK.

His smile was short-lived as he neared the man, whose arms were still raised high, he hoped was Parry.

It wasn't.

Mitch stepped forward and inspected the body of the other man. Again he was disappointed.

Turning, he asked, 'Where's Parry?'

'Honest, mister, I ain't seen him since we got here,' the man answered, his voice as shaky as his body.

'You seen Josh or Maria?' Mitch asked.

'We ain't seen no one 'cept for you fellas.'

Mitch grunted.

At that moment Beefsteak showed up, followed by three other men.

'Tod Jenkins?' Beefsteak's voice was incredulous.

The captured man was silent, but his head sank to his chest.

'Goddamn!' was all Beefsteak could utter.

'You know this man?' Mitch asked.

'Thought I did,' Beefsteak said. 'Seems I don't know him at all!'

'You seen any sign of Josh Winters or Maria?' Mitch asked.

'They lit out north with Doc Mayweather a few hours back,' Beefsteak told him. 'I ain't seen hide nor hair of Parry, though.'

Alarm bells began to ring in Mitch's head, along with the still persistent drumbeats.

'I believe Parry's worked that out and gone after them,' Mitch stated.

'Hell, ol' Josh and them will be in Lubbock by now,' Beefsteak said.

The sun, still low on the eastern horizon, began to shed both light and warmth, and Beefsteak, who hadn't noticed the state of Mitch's head, almost gasped.

'Hell, boy, you got yourself shot up some. You better let me take a looksee.'

'It's just a scratch,' Mitch tried to shrug it off.

'That ain't no scratch, boy, there's some stitchin' needed there, else that purty face'll be a sorry mess. Come on over to the bunkhouse.' Beefsteak was already heading that way as he spoke.

Reluctantly, Mitch followed.

Beefsteak had a pan of water on the pot-bellied stove and was threading a needle. Beside him, on the long table that the hands ate, drank and played cards on, was some clean cotton and a bandage.

'Sit yourself down, boy,' Beefsteak ordered. 'This won't take long but might sting a tad.' Turning to one of the men, he said, 'Where's that whiskey you got stashed away in the belief that no one knows about it?'

'What? I ain't got no —' Clancy answered.

'Go fetch it!' was all Beefsteak said, the menace in his eyes all too apparent to those present.

'Goddamn!' Clancy muttered, and went to his bunk. He returned with a three-quarter-full bottle.

Beefsteak looked at the label. 'Good stuff, eh?' He popped the cork and took a swig. 'Yup, that's good stuff all right.'

He grinned.

'You know what you're doin'?' Mitch asked Beefsteak.

'Boy, I done fixed more broken arms and legs and taken out more bullets than Mr Colt ever fired, an' I can stitch up like an East Coast dressmaker, so don't you fret none.' Beefsteak took another swig of the whiskey and the water began to bubble in the pan.

'Hey,' Clancy grumbled, 'I thought you wanted that for the sewin'?'

Beefsteak grinned. 'I do, and for the sewer, too. That's me. Any objections?'

Clancy was silent.

Beefsteak took the pan off the boiler and set it on the table. He dropped a piece of cotton into it, and a liberal splash of whiskey, which he first ran over the needle.

With hands like leather, Beefsteak removed the cotton cloth, wrung it out and began cleaning Mitch's head wound.

'Ain't too bad,' Beefsteak muttered. 'Four, maybe five stitches'll do it.'

Mitch grabbed the whiskey bottle and

helped himself to two mighty swigs that made his eyes water.

'Do your worst,' he said.

Beefsteak gave a throaty laugh.

13

Amos Kline, Josh Winters's lawyer, was a man of habit.

He awoke every morning at 7 a.m.; was washed and dressed by 7.30; breakfasted at 8.00 and left his small neat house at 8.45 for the walk to his office in the centre of Main Street, Lubbock.

His office was open for business at 9.00 a.m. sharp, come rain or shine, and in this part of Texas it was mainly shine.

A tall, thin, gaunt man with sallow features, he had thinning blond hair, and piercing blue eyes on either side of his beaklike nose.

No one had ever seen him dressed in anything other than an immaculate black suit, white shirt with a stud collar and a bow tie, the colour of which changed daily, and a crimson waistcoat. His handmade boots could be used as a mirror, the shine was that bright. A shine he maintained with aid of spit and a rib bone.

His office was as immaculate as he was. A place for everything and everything in its place was his motto. A motto he followed throughout his life.

His ornate, highly polished oak desk was set in the centre of the room. To his right was a wall covered in shelves upon which volumes of law books sat. At one time or another each of the hundreds of books had been consulted, the information lodged into his precise mind and put to good use.

In the far corner, beside the double-door entrance, was a small stove which, despite the heat, was kept burning.

His first task was to boil some water, open a tin of Arbuckles, and set the coffee on the stove in a highly polished coffee pot.

This performance was repeated three times a day: 9.00 a.m., 1.00 p.m. and 5.00 p.m. The only exceptions were Sunday, a day on which he rested, or when the circuit judge was in town and his presence was required to either defend or prosecute in court.

At 9.15, he poured some coffee into a bone-china cup, placed it on his desk and sat down in his leather-upholstered captain's chair and prepared for his next case.

There was a knock on his door. Amos took out his pocket watch and checked the time. He wasn't expecting anyone until 10 a.m.

He put his watch back in his vest pocket and walked to the door. He saw two people through the frosted glass: one female and one male.

He opened the door and surprise, followed by sorrow, flitted across his face.

There could only be one reason Maria had turned up at his office. Holding out his hand, Amos said, 'I'm so sorry, Maria. Please come in.'

Doc Mayweather took off his battered bowler and the two men, old friends, embraced one another.

'Can I get you a coffee?' Amos asked.

'Not for me,' Maria answered.

'Lou?'

Lou Mayweather could, and often did, drink coffee all day long. 'I could smell the Arbuckles out in the street.' He grinned.

Amos poured a cup for him and ushered the two of them into chairs.

'The will is validated and quite specific,' Amos started. 'You have the, er, death certificate?'

Lou passed over a sealed envelope.

Amos opened it, put on his spectacles and read the document before replacing the certificate back in the envelope.

'That seems to be in order,' he said, then paused for a moment. 'There was no need for you to make the journey here,' he went on. 'I would gladly have come out to the ranch and paid my respects.'

'That would have put your life in danger as well,' Lou said, and went on to explain the situation.

'This must be dealt with by law. Have you informed Sheriff Bates?'

'That's our next call. I'm not sure a town sheriff has the jurisdiction, though,'

Mayweather commented.

'No, he doesn't, but he can call in a US marshal.' 'Where is the, er, deceased?' Amos continued.

'We stayed with Mac Fleetwood last night; he's gone to the undertaker to make the arrangements. We need a temporary grave before we move Josh back to the ranch,' Mayweather said.

'I understand,' Amos said, and took off his spectacles. He turned to Maria. 'My sincere condolences, Maria. I know this is a bad time for you, even without the added complication of your rogue foreman. But you are now the legal owner of the Bar JWM and free to do with it as you wish.'

Maria, who had been silent since her arrival, spoke up.

'I will never sell the Bar JWM,' she stated vehemently. 'Never!'

'You have no need to,' Amos assured her. 'Josh has — had — great faith in your judgement and with the exception of one man, had great faith in your ranch hands. Once this, er, situation, is dispatched, all will be well.' A smile creased Amos's gaunt features, a smile of encouragement.

Latham Parry had slept for an hour or so out in the open. The early morning had been cold, but warm fingers of sunlight began to heat up the day.

He was convinced that Doc Mayweather, along with Maria and Josh Winters, had come to Lubbock having got wind of his plans to take over the ranch. The note from Maria must have, somehow, reached Doc Mayweather.

He had no men, he had little ammunition. What he did have was an insatiable urge to succeed in killing the man who had ruined his brother's life and to take everything he ever owned. The only way he could do that was to make sure Josh and the woman were dead. Then, all he had to do was ride back to the Bar JWM and stake his claim.

He'd see enough of Lubbock in his earlier recce to know it was a bustling town; his presence should raise no eyebrows. Finding Winters should be no problem if he played his cards right, and the best place to start would be the saloon.

First he needed coffee, plenty of coffee, and ham and eggs and sourdough wouldn't go amiss, either.

Parry stood, stretched his stiff and aching limbs, then he saddled up. Parry's horse whinnied.

'Don't worry, boy, I ain't forgot you. Water and barley as soon as we hit town.'

Placing his left boot into the stirrup, he mounted up, pulled his Stetson down tight, and walked his mount slowly towards Lubbock.

Beefsteak was as good as his word. After ten minutes Mitch's wound had been cleaned and sewn up with a minimum of pain.

'There ya go,' Beefsteak said, tying off the cotton thread. 'Good as new an' a nice battle scar to impress the ladies.' Beefsteak chuckled.

''Preciate it,' Mitch said. 'Now I gotta ride north to Lubbock. I figure Parry has gone after Maria and the doc, an' he ain't gone there to wish 'em well.'

'Boys an' me'll ride with ya,' Beefsteak stated.

'No,' Mitch replied. 'I need you to stay here and guard the Bar JWM. Possession bein' nine tenths of the law, so to speak. If'n I fail, Parry will return here, an' you must not let that sonuver get his hands on the ranch.'

Beefsteak was silent for a moment; he glanced at his companions, and then at Mitch. He nodded slowly.

'Guess you're right, son,' Beefsteak said, reluctantly.

'I'll need a fresh mount and all the ammunition you can spare,' Mitch said, standing a little unsteadily.

'We can do that, but first, we eat,' Beefsteak replied. 'You ain't goin' nowhere on an empty stomach.'

'No time for that,' Mitch said.

'Make time, savvy?' Beefsteak smiled.

Within ten minutes, Mitch was tucking hungrily into ham and eggs, a chunk of bread and the best coffee he'd had in a long time.

He finished the meal and drained the coffee, all but smacking his lips.

'Guess I needed that,' he said.

'Horse is ready and there's ammo in the saddle-bags. Good luck, young'un. You get them back here safely, you hear?' Beefsteak shook Mitch's hand warmly.

'I sure will,' Mitch replied, and left the bunkhouse.

Outside, a black mustang snorted as Mitch mounted up. 'Easy boy, easy.' As Mitch stroked its neck, the horse calmed down and accepted its rider.

Without looking back, Mitch left the Bar JWM at a canter, his thoughts now totally on Latham Parry.

As Parry rode into Lubbock, Maria and Doc Mayweather entered the office of the undertaker.

Maria stared at the body of Josh, dressed and laid out ready for the coffin. She thought he looked peaceful and, at last, with no pain creasing his features.

She wiped a small tear away with her

gloved hand and took a deep breath as her body trembled.

'My condolences, ma'am. I know this is a hard time for you. If you'd like to view the coffins ...' The undertaker left the sentence unfinished, as he ushered Maria and the doc into a side room.

The room was lit by the soft, flickering glow of candles, giving just enough light to see that there were several coffins, from plain pine to ornately decorated mahogany. Some had lids that were split in two, one side being left open to reveal the interior of padded cloth of various colours.

It was all too much for Maria to bear; she turned to Doc Mayweather, looked pleadingly into his eyes.

Mayweather nodded, instantaneously understanding her. 'Don't worry, I'll sort the arrangements,' he said gently.

Maria mouthed a *thank you*, and left the room.

Ten minutes later, the doc and the undertaker returned.

'Maria, I've provisionally arranged for

the interment to be at noon, tomorrow. I hope that meets with your approval?'

Maria merely nodded. She didn't take her eyes off the peaceful face of the man she had loved all these years.

Holding her elbow, Doc Mayweather gently led her out of the funeral parlour and back to Doc Fleetwood's.

Parry had checked his horse into the livery. He gave the stable hand a dollar and told him to feed, water and groom his mount, as he figured he might have a hard ride back to the Bar JWM later that day.

He grabbed his saddle-bag, tossed it over his shoulder and made his way to a small café. He sat at a table by the window, where he had a good view of the main street.

'What'll it be, mister?' a surly waitress asked.

'Breakfast, an' plenty of it,' Parry replied.

'Coffee?'

'You bet.'

The food arrived and Parry started eating like a man who'd not eaten in weeks.

The waitress snorted in disgust, but one look from the manic eyes of the customer sent her scurrying back to the relative safety of the kitchen.

Cal Morgan could stand it no further.

'Look,' he said to the assembled men, 'nothing is going to happen here and, despite what Mitch said, I intend to ride out to the Bar JWM.'

He paused, waiting for any comments. The only person to answer was Ellie-Rae.

'I'm coming with you,' she said.

This brought an immediate chorus of disapproval.

She glared at the assembled company. 'I can ride and shoot better than any of you,' she spat. 'Are you suggesting I shouldn't go because I'm a woman?'

There was silence.

'That's settled then,' she said, trying hard not to smile.

'I still think —' Cal started, but didn't get the chance to finish.

'You've still got a crippled leg; what do you hope to achieve on your own?' Ellie-Rae said, with a steely glint in her eye.

'OK, you win. Let's git goin',' he conceded.

The mayor cleared his throat. 'Get all the ammo you need,' he said. 'Town council will foot the bill.'

Cal got to his feet and made his way outside, followed by Ellie.

'I'll bring the horses round,' Ellie said. 'You sort the ammunition, OK?'

Cal nodded and followed the mayor to the hardware store.

Ten minutes later, Ellie returned, mounted on her magnificent palomino and leading Cal's sorrel.

Cal threw a saddle-bag across his horse's rump, clambered aboard, and they set off for the Bar JWM.

Mitch Evans reined in on the outskirts of Lubbock. It looked peaceful with townsfolk going about their business. He walked his horse on.

His first port of call was the sheriff's office, where he found out for sure that Maria and the doc were in town and the bonus of where they were staying.

Mitch tied his horse to the picket fence outside Doc Fleetwood's house and knocked on the door.

Inside, the three people froze. Mayweather put a finger to his lips and picked up the Colt lying on the kitchen table.

Walking stealthily on the balls of his feet, Mayweather went towards the front door.

'Who's there?' he called.

'It's Mitch, Mitch Evans.'

Mayweather slipped the bolt and flung the front door open, the relief on his face all too evident.

'You might want to lower that pistol a tad,' Mitch said with a grin.

Flustered, the doc suddenly remembered he was holding a gun. 'Sorry, sorry. Come on in, good to see you.' He ushered Mitch inside, then locked and bolted the door. 'Go on through,' he added.

'Maria, Mac, this here is Mitch Evans,

brother of the late Brad Evans.'

Mac shook Mitch's hand, and Maria smiled. 'He was a fine man with a lovely family,' Maria said.

Mitch removed his hat and gave a slight bow to Maria.

'What news do you have?' Mayweather asked.

'Parry and his men attacked the Bar JWM,' Mitch began. 'They failed. I think he figured where Maria and Josh were headed, so I believe he's in town. He needs to kill you both before he can take over the ranch.'

'Josh is already dead, Mitch,' Mayweather said. 'He died peacefully in his sleep. We thought Parry might try something, so we brought him here as Maria is his sole heir.'

'I'm so sorry to hear that,' Mitch said. He didn't know what else to say.

'What are you going to do when you find Latham Parry?' Doc Mayweather asked.

Mitch looked Mayweather in the eye and said simply, 'I'm going to kill him.'

Mitch was expecting objections, but there were none, just a silence.

'I don't want you all to stay here. I've spoken with the sheriff, and we agreed it's too dangerous here. I think Parry has gone over the edge and is likely to do anything.' Mitch looked at each of them in turn.

'Do you have any weapons?' he asked.

It was Mac Fleetwood who answered. 'I got several rifles and handguns,' he said. 'Some folks don't pay in dollars.' He grinned and winked and opened a cupboard to display an arsenal of assorted weapons.

'Hell! You got enough there to arm an army,' Lou Mayweather said.

'Choose your weapons carefully,' Mitch said. 'Some of them guns look as if they ain't been used in years.' He picked up a Winchester. 'This one looks fine,' he said and handed it to Doc Mayweather.

Mac Fleetwood selected two more rifles and two handguns. 'There's plenty of ammunition there, too,' he said.

'OK. I hope you won't need to use

them,' Mitch said. 'I'll check the back entrance. When I give the signal, follow me, OK?'

They nodded their agreement.

Mitch checked the rear of the building. It was all clear and he waved an arm. One by one, with Maria in the middle, the three left the house and followed Mitch down an alleyway. Mitch turned into a gated backyard and knocked on the door of a building. When it opened the four of them hurried inside.

'Guess you know the sheriff,' Mitch said as the door closed. 'Parry won't think to look here. He'll soon find out where you two were stayin', an' that'll be his focus. I'm going to have a walk around town,' he went on. 'Parry doesn't know me, so he'll not recognize me.'

'Thing is,' Doc Mayweather piped up, 'you don't know him, either.'

Cal and Ellie-Rae ground their horses to a halt outside the bunkhouse of the Bar JWM.

Beefsteak had had his rifle trained on

them since they came into view. Then he recognized Cal and the woman, although he couldn't put a name to her.

Cal, whose leg was healing up some, was still stiff, but he could put weight on it, almost leapt from his saddle.

'Cal! What in hell — Sorry, ma'am. What you doin' here?' Beefsteak asked.

'I came to give Mitch a hand,' Cal replied.

'Well, he ain't here,' Beefsteak said.

'What? Where is he?' Ellie-Rae interjected, concern on her face.

'He rode on up to Lubbock. We reckon Parry headed there, chasing after Mr Winters and Maria,' Beefsteak said, matter of factly.

'When did he leave?' Cal asked.

'I'd say about three hours ago. He'll be there now. Come on inside. We can't be sure if Parry will return or not, so it's not safe to be out in the open.' Beefsteak stepped aside and motioned them into the bunkhouse.

'There's five of us here, should be enough to manage Parry — should he return. He's alone now. His little gang were either killed or ran off. Coffee?' Beefsteak picked up the pot and two tin mugs. Without waiting for an answer he filled the mugs and handed one to each of them.

'I'm going up to Lubbock,' Cal stated.

'Ain't no point in you goin' there,' Beefsteak told him. 'One way or another, it'll be over before you get up there. You're more useful stayin' here and helping us guard the Bar JWM.'

'Makes sense, Cal,' Ellie-Rae said.

'There's law in Lubbock. Ain't like Calvary. Mitch won't be alone,' Beefsteak added.

Cal was torn in two: go or stay?

It was Ellie-Rae who decided. 'We'll stay and help out here.'

Beefsteak smiled. 'OK. I got a key to the house, I suggest you go there, Miss …?'

'Call me Ellie.'

'Miss Ellie. Ain't safe out here and if you use one of the upstairs rooms, you get a good view. House is south-facin', so a rear room is best.'

'And you are?' Ellie asked.

'Folks call me Beefsteak.' He handed Ellie the key to the front door.

'Cal, you come with me, I want you in the barn, up in the hayloft. I'll let my men know where you are; don't want no accidental shootin', do we?' Beefsteak broke into a hearty laugh.

Parry had lingered over his fifth cup of coffee. He stomped out his cigarette, drained the cup and left a couple of dollars on the table as he left.

He knew the saddle-bag over his shoulder marked him out as a stranger, but it couldn't be helped. To his left was the sheriff's office and on his right a saloon, and already he could hear laughter and the tinkling of an out-of-tune piano.

At the counter, he ordered a beer and a whiskey chaser. His presence didn't seem to raise too many eyebrows, just an occasional glance in his direction.

He sipped at his beer as he looked at

the mirror behind the bar and took in the patrons sitting at tables.

'New in town?' the barkeep asked, passing the time of day.

'Yeah, just rode in on my way back to the Bar JWM,' Parry replied, thinking the more information he gave, the more he might receive.

'Travelled far?' the 'keep asked.

'Just here an' about; been checking on getting some new stock.'

'Got yourself a spread, then?' The 'keep started polishing another glass that didn't need it.

'Hell, no,' Parry replied. He paused, thinking if he gave out more information, the 'keep might open up on any gossip he'd heard. 'I'm foreman down to the Bar JWM.'

The bartender stopped polishing the glass he was holding and his mouth fell open. He gulped.

'Sorry to hear about ol' man Winters,' he said.

'What!' Parry's surprise and interest were apparent on his face. 'What about him?' he asked.

'Sorry, mister, but he's dead. Over to the undertaker's now. Rumour has it funeral's tomorrow.'

Latham Parry managed to keep a smile off his face — just! He took off his Stetson and managed to portray sadness.

'Anyone come here with him?' he asked tentatively.

The barkeep leaned forward in a conspiratorial way and said, 'Well, I heard his housekeeper and the ol' doc from Calvary came in last night. They're stayin' with Doc Fleetwood,' he said.

Parry drained his beer and thanked the barkeep.

'Be seein' you,' the 'keep said.

Parry smiled in return. A smile that sent a shiver down the barkeep's back.

After ensuring that both Maria and Doc Mayweather were secure in the sheriff's house, Mitch left with Doc Fleetwood, to have a look around town.

'How you gonna recognize this varmint?' Doc Fleetwood asked.

'Don't rightly know, Doc. I'll just take a walk round town, maybe call in a saloon or two. Parry won't know me either,' Mitch answered with a grin.

'I'll leave you here,' Fleetwood said. 'Prob'ly got a whole stack of belly-achers waitin' on me. You take care. I'll look in on Maria and Lou later on.'

The two men parted. Mitch looked up and down Main Street, pondering on which direction to take, decided north, then ambled along the boardwalk.

The town seemed to be growing bigger by the day.

Mitch stopped outside one ladies' fashion shop and stared in wonder at the dresses displayed in the window. He whistled as he saw the prices. More than he earned in a year!

Shaking his head in both wonder and amazement, Mitch walked on. Soon he came to a stop outside a small café. The aroma of bacon and fresh coffee assailed his nostrils, reminding him he hadn't eaten since a hurried breakfast.

He entered and sat at a table set next

to a large window. He ordered steak, onions, mashed potato and gravy, as well as coffee, and sat keeping an eye on Main Street.

It took less than ten minutes to devour the mountain of food and three cups of coffee.

'Some pie, mister?' the waitress asked as she cleared the table.

'Ma'am, that was the finest meal I had in a long time an' I'm fit to bustin',' Mitch said and smiled.

The waitress/owner, a woman of middle years, smiled and seemed to flush at the compliment.

'Mind me askin', ma'am, you get many strangers in today?'

'Get them all the time,' she answered. 'Town's growin' faster than ever lately. Had a few in today, one in particular I didn't take a fancy to. Mean-looking critter if you ask me. Just sat staring out of the window.'

'What did he look like?' Mitch asked.

'Dark-skinned, obviously a cowboy,

212

black lank hair. Looked like he hadn't washed in a few days, if you ask me. And he had the meanest brown eyes I ever did see, sent shivers down my spine.' She stopped and seemed to inwardly shudder at the thought.

Mitch took out a few dollars and placed them in her hand. 'I thank you, ma'am.' Tipping his Stetson, Mitch left the café.

It was late afternoon and already the stores were beginning to take stock of the day's trading, bringing in goods from the boardwalk and preparing to close for the night.

Where the hell would a man like Parry hang out? And what did he hope to achieve?

Mitch's thoughts were interrupted by the sound of a badly tuned piano. Looking across the street, he saw a saloon.

He stepped off the boardwalk, crossed the dusty street and entered the saloon.

The air was stale and a fug of smoke

hung in the air like low-lying clouds. There were perhaps twenty or thirty people scattered around the large room. Along the far wall a bar stretched from corner to corner. Mitch walked towards it and ordered a beer. Taking a mouthful, Mitch scanned the faces of the men seated at rough wooden tables.

None of them seemed to match the vague description he had been given. Maybe he should try another bar, he thought. But then he descided he'd stake out Doc Fleetwood's place instead. He figured that, if he was after Maria and Doc Mayweather, he'd keep a low profile and wait until it was dark before making any move.

Little did Mitch realize how close he was to the truth.

14

The sun dropped in the sky like a stone down a well.

The clear blue sky quickly turned to purple, then black and the landscape which had been bathed in a crimson hue became silver-grey as the moon's reflected light took over for the night.

In less than an hour Lubbock became a ghost town as the shops closed, and townsfolk made their way home for supper. The only signs of life were the street-lighter and the soft glow of lantern light coming from the various saloons up and down Main Street.

Mitch had positioned himself in an alleyway opposite Doc Fleetwood's surgery, where, hidden in the dark shadows, he had an uninterrupted view.

For over an hour there had been only the occasional passer-by. Mitch took out his hunter and checked on the time.

Eight o'clock.

No sooner had he put his watch back in his vest pocket than more people started to come down Main. Some on horseback, probably from the outlying ranches and farms, but most on foot. Within the space of five minutes Lubbock came to life again.

It was as if some unheard signal had been sent out.

Mitch became more alert; he tried to study each man as he passed by, but in the poor light, it was almost impossible to assess features, especially on the scant information he had.

So he waited.

Latham Parry had used what little charm he had in an attempt to make a friend of the liveryman. Conversation was easy on subjects such as whiskey and horses, both of which were readily available.

After an hour of idle chitchat and a bottle of cheap rotgut — most of which was consumed by the liveryman — Parry could see that the man was falling into a drunken stupor.

216

Parry stubbed out his cigarette. It was time to put his plan into action.

Behind the livery stable was a small barn where hay and feed were kept. Ideal for his purposes: to create a diversion.

Methodically, he saddled up his mount and gave it a sack of barley to keep the animal calm. Next, he reached into his saddle-bag and carefully removed its contents.

He unwrapped the linen parcel and removed three sticks of dynamite. He tied the sticks together and inserted a short fuse.

He put the sticks back into his saddle-bag, took the feed sack off his horse and mounted up. He slowly walked the horse to the feed shack, struck a lucifer and tossed it inside.

Parry waited for a few minutes, making sure the match had caught the fuse, and then cantered off down a side alley.

He made his way to the side of the nearest saloon and shouted: 'Fire! Fire!' and waited for the response.

He didn't have to wait long.

The biggest fear of any town in the West was fire. Lubbock was no exception. Within minutes men ran into the saloon and passed the word on. Soon, Main Street was packed with men all looking for smoke or flames.

'There it is!' a voice shouted and a finger pointed towards the livery.

The bucket store was opened and men ran to the livery to form a chain from the water trough. The feed shack was well ablaze and as the men arrived, the roof caved in, sending sparks high into the air, bringing the possibility of the fire spreading quickly.

Mitch heard the ruckus and cautiously stepped into the street. He caught the smell of smoke and saw sparks rising on the thermal of the fire. He could also see the bucket chain forming, so there was little point in him joining the organized chaos.

Everyone's attention was focused on the fire, including Mitch's.

He failed to see the lone rider walking his mount down Main Street

218

away from the livery.

Parry rode down the side of Doc Fleetwood's surgery, dismounted and calmly lit a cigarette. He took out some more dynamite, touched the cigarette to the fuse, broke a side window and tossed the explosives inside.

He mounted up quickly, steered his horse to the end of the alleyway, turned a sharp right and galloped out of Lubbock.

The force of the blast blew Mitch off his feet and he landed heavily in the dirt.

Slightly dizzy, and gasping for breath, he got to his knees and stared blankly at the gap that used to be a surgery.

Flames were licking at the walls that remained and Mitch saw that he was surrounded by shattered wood. As he stared, what was left of the roof collapsed, sending up a shower of sparks into the night sky.

Mitch cursed as he suddenly realized that Parry was smarter than he'd given him credit for.

Shaking his head, trying to get the

ringing out of his ears, Mitch got to his feet.

Hell! Doc Fleetwood!

Mitch ran towards the still burning building, shielding his face with one hand, but it was impossible to see anything in the raging inferno.

'Mitch? You OK?'

Turning quickly with his Colt levelled, Mitch looked into the face of the old doctor.

'Jeez, Doc! I thought you were inside.'

'Well, I woulda bin, but Mrs Jenkins decided it was high time she gave birth. A little girl.' Doc Fleetwood smiled.

'I better check on Doc Mayweather and Maria. Parry already made one diversion, this could be a second,' Mitch said.

Doc Fleetwood was silent for a moment, then, 'I reckon he thinks we were all in there, Mitch. I also reckon he's high-tailed it back to the Bar JWM to stake his claim.'

'Doc, you go stay with Maria and the doc. Tell 'em I'm heading back to the Bar JWM — pronto!'

Without another word, Mitch raced for his mount and set off.

Latham Parry had a good head start. His mount, fed and watered, was fresh and eager for the gallop.

Parry's face had the look of a maniac. If he wasn't already over the edge, he was pretty close to it.

He had one thought on his mind and one thought only: to take control of the Bar JWM and avenge the mutilation of his now dead brother.

Nothing else mattered.

As he rode, his brain was working overtime. He was one man; he could only guess at how many of the hands were on the ranch when he left. He knew of three for certain sure, but there could be more.

He knew he'd have to slip on to the ranch and pick them off one by one. With the element of surprise, he could see no problem in achieving his goal. With Josh and Maria dead, there was no one to stop him and he'd soon get his own men to run the ranch. His only problem was how the hands on the cattle drive would react when they returned.

He would worry about that later.

His mind then moved on to Mitch Evans: the fly in the ointment. He was possibly the one man who could ruin his plans.

Maybe, he thought, he should have taken care of him first. But where the hell was he?

It was just after one in the morning when Parry reined in. Steam rose from the body of his horse in the chill night air. He had just crested the rise that led down to the ranch house of the Bar JWM.

The light from the moon wasn't bright enough to get a clear view, as high-flying clouds scudded across the sky, momentarily blocking out the moonlight altogether.

Despite his impatience to get the job done, Parry knew it made more sense to wait for dawn. He had to see how many, if any, men were down there, and pinpoint their positions.

He knew that taking out the first man would be easy, as they wouldn't be expecting trouble, but after that ...?

He had at least three hours to kill, so he walked his horse to a nearby hollow, where there was plenty of grass and he'd be out of sight from the ranch.

He found a comfortable spot, lay down and pulled his Stetson over his eyes. Within seconds he fell asleep.

'We must get back to the ranch,' Maria said, gathering up her shawl.

'Maria, we have the funeral in the morning,' Doc Mayweather said.

'No! We take Josh back to the Bar JWM, he'll be buried on his ranch,' Maria stated firmly. 'Knowing that that despicable man has been here to kill us, we must get back and do what we can.'

'Maria, it will take us hours to get back with the buggy. Let's wait until dawn at least. The trail is treacherous enough and I'm not as fit as I used to be. Whatever happens will have happened before we get there.' Doc Mayweather was almost pleading.

Maria pondered this. 'I suppose you are right, I'm sorry. OK, we leave at dawn. Agreed?'

'Agreed,' Mayweather said, his relief evident in his tone.

'I suggest you folks get some shuteye now,' the sheriff chipped in. 'I got to go back and make sure both fires are out. We don't want the town to go up in smoke! I'll wake you come dawn.'

Mitch reached the Bar JWM and, unlike Parry, had stuck to the main trail. He paused briefly, listening intently for any sounds coming from the ranch.

All was quiet; and all he had to do now was ride in without getting shot at.

He walked his horse on. As he approached the barn a voice rang out.

'Hold it right there, mister!'

Mitch reined in and put both arms in the air.

'It's me, Mitch Evans,' he called out.

'Good to see you, Mitch,' the voice

called out again.

'Cal? What in tarnation …?'

'You didn't think we'd leave you to fight this on your own, did ya?' Cal said with a grin.

'We?' Mitch said. 'Who else is here?'

'Miss Ellie-Rae is over to the house. That woman doesn't take 'no' for an answer. Bring your horse in, Mitch, and tell us what went on in Lubbock.'

Mitch tried hard to keep a smile off his face, and failed. He dismounted, led the horse into the barn, then told the astonished listeners what had happened in Lubbock.

'So Maria and Doc Mayweather are fine,' he told them. 'But I'm convinced Parry headed back here after he blew up the surgery there.'

'Seth,' Beefsteak piped up, 'you an' Marky get on over to the ranch house and check Miss Ellie is OK. You stay with her. One of you keep a lookout from the upstairs windows at the rear. Brad, you take the bunkhouse, we'll guard the barn. That should give us a good all-round view.'

No one argued with Beefsteak's plan. In fact, no one ever argued with Beefsteak.

As the sun began its relentless climb over the eastern horizon, Parry woke up as if an alarm had sounded.

Rubbing his eyes, he sat up and, for a second, wondered where the hell he was.

Instantly he was alert. He grabbed his Winchester and army-issue telescope and crawled up the small rise. He first checked the ranch house, then the barn. As the light grew brighter, he had a clear view of the compound. To the right, the ranch house, next to that the corral, then the bunkhouse and, finally, the huge barn.

From his vantage point he could see no movement and was about to put the 'scope away, when two armed men walked out of the barn, heading towards the ranch house.

Dropping the telescope, Parry grabbed his rifle. He took two deep breaths as he sighted down the barrel. He held in the third breath and squeezed the trigger.

The explosion of the rifle shattered

the early morning silence and his horse whinnied at the shock.

Parry cocked the rifle again and let off another shot.

He took up the 'scope again and looked at the two men lying in the dirt. One was still moving — just.

'Two down,' Parry muttered. 'How many more to go?'

'Goddamn!' Mitch yelled. 'He is here!'

'Marky's still moving,' Beefsteak yelled, and ran to the barn door.

'Beefsteak, wait! You'll get yourself shot,' Cal called.

'I ain't leaving Marky out there,' Beefsteak replied. But before he could react, another shot rang out.

Marky stopped moving.

'Damn that sonuvver! He done killed a wounded man.' Beefsteak was almost beside himself with rage.

Mitch was thoughtful. He'd seen the way the two men had fallen and that gave him an idea of the shooter's whereabouts.

'Can I borrow that Sharps, Beefsteak?'

Mitch asked.

'What in hell do you want my gun for?' Beefsteak asked.

'I reckon I know roughly where Parry might be. I aim to cut round and outflank him, with your help.' Looking Beefsteak straight in the eye, Mitch explained his theory.

'That's a pretty wide area up there,' Cal said. 'What if I come round from the other side?'

'Cal, when the shootin' starts I want you to make it to the ranch house and protect Ellie-Rae, cos if I fail …'

Mitch didn't need to finish the sentence. Cal just nodded.

Reluctantly, Beefsteak handed over the heavy Sharps rifle, and a box of ammo. 'You look after it now, and yourself,' Beefsteak said.

Mitch smiled. Heading for a cloth-covered window in the far side of the barn, he made his exit.

'Well, you heard the man,' Cal said. 'Let's get into position and give Mitch some covering fire.'

228

As Mitch landed in the soft earth another shot rang out. It seemed random, like Parry was just aiming at the barn. Mitch couldn't get a direction from the explosive sound of the rifle being fired, its echo seemed to be all around him, but he was sure it came from some way up the rise.

Immediately a fusillade of shots erupted from the barn. Beefsteak and Cal had edged their way out of the main entrance and were firing blindly. At first Parry kept his head down, but as soon as he realized the shots were nowhere near him, he raised both his head and the Winchester.

As he sighted he could see part of one leg jutting out from the side of the barn. Holding his breath, he squeezed the trigger.

The leg disappeared and Parry knew he'd made a hit.

Beefsteak wheeled to the right, slamming into the barn wall.

'Goddamn! I been hit,' he called out through gritted teeth.

Cal managed to drag the big man back inside the barn and lean him up against a bale of hay.

'Don't look none too serious,' Cal said as he cut through Beefsteak's trousers. 'Just a flesh wound,' he added with a smile.

'Sure stings a mite,' Beefsteak moaned.

'I gotta get to Miss Ellie,' Cal said. 'Patch him up real tight,' he told one of the hands. 'You'll live, Beefsteak.'

Cal was no fool. He guessed from the wound that the angle of shot was some 45 degrees from the front of the barn. Studying the ground between him and the ranch house, and hoping his guess was right, he left the barn and turned sharp left, heading for the bunkhouse. Running zigzag style, he made it safely with no shots being fired.

He knew the next dash would be more dangerous. He had to pass behind the corral and that would surely bring him into the view of Parry.

There were about a dozen horses in the corral; with luck they might shield him.

After taking a deep breath Cal raced to the side of the ranch house, crouching as low as he could. Again, no shots were fired; he made it to the rear of the house and knocked on the back door.

There was no immediate reaction, so he knocked louder. Cal then heard the metallic click of a gun being cocked.

'Who is it?' a female voice called out.

'It's me, Cal, let me in.'

Bolts were pulled back and the lock clicked as Ellie opened the door.

'What's happening? I heard all the shots,' Ellie asked.

'We lost two men, and Beefsteak caught a slug in his leg, but he'll be OK,' Cal responded.

'And Mitch?' she asked, wringing her hands.

'Mitch figured roughly where Parry was shooting from, and he's gone after him,' Cal said. 'You're kinda sweet on him, ain't you?' he added.

Ellie-Rae didn't answer, merely lowered her eyes, which was answer enough for Cal.

'I want you to stay in the centre of the house. I'll be upstairs at one of the front windows, that way I can see anyone approaching and I'll know you're safe. Can I take these?' Cal pointed to a box of slugs.

'Sure. There's a whole bunch of ammunition here,' Ellie-Rae answered.

'Make sure the back door is relocked and bolted, OK?' Cal told her. Then he left the kitchen and raced upstairs.

Parry hadn't seen any movement for the last ten minutes or so and it did cross his mind that there might be only two men down there; he knew for sure that they were dead.

He racked his brains to recall who should be there. With most of the crew on the cattle drive there would only be a skeleton crew left on the ranch. Beefsteak would be there for sure: he remembered the man telling his assistant to take care of the chuck wagon for the drive.

So who else would be there?

Even though he was foreman, he couldn't for the life of him think who might have stayed behind. Most of the men were of no interest to him, were merely a means to an end.

An end he intended to bring about today.

Raising his head above the rise again, he took out his 'scope and scanned the area, starting with the ranch house, moving from window to window, looking for the slightest movement.

Then he caught something. A brief flash of light. Someone was in one of the upstairs rooms.

Parry smiled to himself. He wasn't sure if the ranch house was within firing range but, with no wind to speak of, it was worth a shot.

He wiped a bead of sweat from his forehead, drying his hand on his shirt before sighting down the long barrel again.

At this distance he could not see anything inside the house with the naked eye, but he was certain someone was on lookout.

He lightly fingered the trigger, gently began to squeeze until he heard the familiar click as the hammer engaged with the shell-casing. It all seemed to go in slow motion: the kick-back from the Winchester pushed into his right shoulder; the smell of cordite hit his nostrils like an old friend even as the slug left the barrel.

He could almost see the bullet flying through the air to its target.

Parry couldn't hear the tinkling of the glass as it exploded inwards, but in his head he heard it.

He waited.

There was no return fire from the ranch house, but two shots came from the barn; Parry managed to pinpoint the muzzle flash of one of them.

The shooting was erratic and nowhere near his position, so he took careful aim once more and fired.

This time he could hear the shriek as the bullet found its target.

Another one down. So, there had been four men down there at least, he thought. How many more?

Cal realized his mistake in an instant. How could he be so foolish as to light up a cigarette! But his nerves were jangling. He was, after all, a rannie not a gunman and felt he needed a smoke.

The slug had caught him high in the shoulder, midway between his head and shoulder, spinning him back in a twisting motion and he landed heavily on the carpeted floor.

His left hand immediately felt for the wound and he withdrew it to see how much blood there was. He stared at a small spot on his palm and breathed a sigh of relief just as Ellie-Rae burst through the door brandishing her rifle.

She looked down at Cal, horror written on her face. 'You hit?'

Cal stood, winced slightly at the movement, but answered, 'Just a flesh wound, it's nothing. Hey, keep away from that window!'

From his position Mitch could now pinpoint roughly where Parry was holed up. He edged forward, keeping low, then stopped as the second shot rang out.

In the blink of an eye Mitch caught sight of a flash. He wasn't sure if it was a muzzle flash or sunlight reflecting off a gun barrel. Either way, it was Parry.

Mitch quickly brought the Sharps up to bear, pushing it tightly against his shoulder. With a range of over 800 yards and enough power to down a buffalo, anyone hit by a Sharps stood very little chance of surviving.

Sighting down the 32-inch barrel, feeling the weight of the eight-pound weapon, Mitch waited for Parry to raise his head again.

Then he heard the sound of horses thundering down the trail. 'Shit!' he muttered. Was it Parry's men, or—

There was no time to waste. Throwing caution to the wind, Mitch ran forward.

Parry heard the approaching horses too, and he ran to the opposite side of the hollow, his 'scope to his eye.

'Damn!' he breathed. For in the approaching buggy sat Doc Mayweather and that damned Gonzalez woman!

Parry saw red. He forgot all about the barn and ranch house and focused his maniacal attention on one thing and one thing only: *kill that woman.*

He settled himself at the base of a cottonwood and took aim. So intense was his anger that, instead of his usual careful preparation, he yanked at the trigger. His aim was poor, but didn't go unnoticed by Doc Mayweather. He veered the reins to the left and went off-trail over bumpy ground. Maria held on tightly, for she was being tossed around like a cork in a river.

Parry cursed and fired again. This time he caught one of the ponies a glancing shot and the animal panicked, grinding to a halt as the other horse kept galloping.

Mayweather lost control and the buggy slewed to the left. Both he and Maria were tossed to the ground like rag dolls.

Parry kept firing, but his shots were wild: the shooting of a madman.

Mitch reached the far side of the

hollow and covered Parry with the Sharps.

'Hold it right there, Parry,' he shouted out. 'Drop that rifle!'

Parry froze; there was no way he was going to give up.

'Toss that rifle aside,' Mitch ordered.

Parry did exactly that: using his left hand he threw the rifle to the ground. At the same time his right hand went for his Colt.

He was quick, but his shot missed Mitch by inches.

Mitch didn't hesitate. He squeezed the trigger of the Sharps, the recoil of the weapon nearly knocking him off his feet.

The .52-calibre slug hit Parry like a sledgehammer. The man was thrown back five feet, slamming into the trunk of the cottonwood in a fountain of blood. Slowly, his crumpled body slid to the ground, the look of surprise and hatred still etched on his face.

Mitch ignored the twitching body as he ran to the crest of the hollow to see what had happened to the buggy.

He caught sight of Doc Mayweather, 200 yards away, beginning to sit up, obviously winded.

Ten feet from the doc he saw Maria lying still in the grass. Mayweather made his way to her side and lifted her head on to his lap as Mitch raced down towards them.

'Mitch! Am I glad to see you,' Mayweather said with a smile. 'She's just stunned, no bullet wound,' he added, relief evident in his voice.

'Glad to hear it, Doc. Had me worried there. Wait here, I'll get a wagon to pick you up.'

Mitch turned and ran back to the ranch.

Beefsteak had him covered in an instant, then, fortunately recognized Mitch.

Cal also saw him and instinctively knew Parry was finished. He and Ellie-Rae rushed out of the house into the compound, where they greeted Mitch.

Ellie couldn't help herself; she flung her arms around his neck, kissing him on the cheek at the same time. Mitch didn't want to let her go, but forced himself to tell Cal to team up a wagon.

'Maria and the doc are over yonder, and I think I saw a coffin by their buggy.'

'Sure thing, Mitch. And, glad you're OK. Is Parry …?'

'He won't be causing any more trouble this side of hell,' Mitch replied sombrely.

Maria recovered fully, with only a small lump on the side of her head. Doc Mayweather patched up both Cal and Beefsteak, and everyone relaxed for the first time in the three days that had seemed like an eternity.

The feelings between Ellie-Rae and Mitch Evans were quite mutual and Maria, now owner of the richest ranch this side of Texas, decided she'd found her new foreman.

Mitch was flattered, but his answer was guarded.

'Depends what the wife-to-be has to say,' he said, and grinned sheepishly.

Ellie-Rae didn't have to answer. She threw her arms around his neck and they kissed passionately.

The Bar JWM had a new foreman.